10 Pretty Cool

Little Horror Stories

Daniel J. Kaminski

Ten Pretty Cool Little Horror Stories

Cover art and design by Jennifer French

For two of the true masters of the short story, Edgar Allen Poe and Ray Bradbury, whose imagination, style, and instruction were the inspiration for this book of stories.

Table of Contents

Normal is an illusion. What is normal to the spider is chaos to the fly.

- Charles Addams

Most grownups don't want to see or accept such things. But kids know they really do happen.

- Teddy, from the story, *The Merry-Go-Round*

Foreword

There are many who consider Edgar Allen Poe to be the master of the short story. With an easy online search, you can find Poe's rules on writing. One of those rules has to do with length, namely, that a story should be able to be read in one sitting. His classic, *The Tell-Tale Heart*, is considered by numerous literary critics to be the perfect short story. That perfect story is less than 20 paragraphs long. Depending upon the medium from which you read the tale, and the size of the print, that amounts to only three or four pages of brilliant gothic horror.

I've followed Poe's advice here. This is a book of *short* stories. Not only can a tale that I present to you in this collection be read in one sitting; if you like them, the entire collection may be read in one sitting, depending upon whether you have the time on a particular day to knock them all out, or you'd rather binge-watch something on Netflix that day instead. I like to think of these stories as meat and potatoes writing, with a metaphor thrown in here, and some foreshadowing there—serving as garnishes displayed around the plate to give this meal of prose some color, and make it more palatable to you.

Additionally, I've included a brief introduction to each tale. A common question that is posed to writers is where do you get the ideas for the stories that you write? It's a fair question, but the answer may not be so clear.

They might stem from a real-life experience, or perhaps they came from a weird dream that was brought on by eating a bad dinner—like one that included a big bowl of kale. I think the answer mostly comes down to this: writers have to look at people and places, animals, the air, land, and sea, and life in general, in a different way than it appears on the surface. Here's an example: You've heard it said that the optimist sees the glass as half full. The pessimist sees the glass as half empty. But what if you look at the glass and instead see a microscopic civilization in widespread panic over the evaporation of their atmosphere? Their politicians, social scientists, clergy, and engineers are scrambling to find an escape from their pending apocalypse.

There are shades of Dr. Seuss's *Horton Hears a Who* in the above example, except we're talking about a water world instead of life on a dust speck. That's also where stories might come from—the author's take on a theme or subject that's previously been covered by someone else. After all, how many vampire novels and short stories have been written since *Dracula*? I've even got one such story in this collection. By the way, *Dracula* wasn't even the first vampire story. There were several published before Bram Stoker's famous novel.

Each of the introductions includes where the idea for the story came from. I think the introductions are accurate in that regard. Then again, all of the stories may have just been a product of that dreadful bowl of kale.

Okay, so let's get started. Thank you, dear reader, for taking a little time out of your busy day to read these little stories. Glad to see that you opted to join me instead of watching Netflix this evening. Find a nice, cozy place to recline and settle in. Open your mind and let your imagination wander. Don't worry about those strange sounds you may hear from outside in the fog-shrouded night, or that may be coming from that forgotten, shadowy corner of your bedroom closet, or from the darkness directly beneath your bed. It's probably just the howling of the wind, or a creaking floorboard. Well, then again, maybe it is something else. But just pull the covers around you a little closer for protection, and keep the lights on for a little while longer. Always keep in mind that the dawn is coming. You just have to make it through the darkness first.

This story came to me while I was employed in my illustrious career as a civil servant for the State of New Jersey. Contrary to what this fictional tale may intimate, my co-workers and I actually did do our jobs, and didn't spend all our taxpayer-funded work hours looking out the windows and playing Solitaire on our desktops—at least not all of the time. The character of the Pharaoh was based on a real guy who used to work at the parking lot across the street from our building. For all I know, he might still be wandering around there today—haunting the City of Trenton. On an actual historical note, I make reference to the Rodney King verdict in Los Angeles in 1992. At about 2:00 that day, our Director came to everyone's cubicle and told us to shut down and go home. The authorities feared there might be rioting in Trenton in protest of the verdict and wanted people out of town. Our parking lot was three-blocks from the building. Although no riots did occur in Trenton over the verdict, my walk to the parking lot that afternoon was the most eerily quiet, ominous 10 minutes that I ever spent in 28 plus years of working in that City. You've heard it said that truth is stranger than fiction. Sometimes it's also scarier than fiction.

THE PHARAOH OF TRENTON

Well, there I was, sitting in the Detectives Squad Room of the City of Trenton Police Department. Yes, they had found me leaning over the guy with blood all over my clothes and a bloody knife in my hands; but seriously, I did not kill him. Obviously, they didn't believe me. In my bewildered state, I'd waived my right to refuse to answer questions without an attorney there.

I told the cops, "It was his hair. That's how I originally came to give him the nickname. He had this afro ... You probably saw his hairdo when you found his body lying there. Did any of you guys ever see the movie, *The Ten Commandments?*"

I knew it sounded like nervous rambling to them, but I was actually going somewhere with this. "Anyway, Yul Brynner is in the movie. He plays Ramses, the Pharaoh. I think it was Ramses... it definitely wasn't Cheops. No, that was a guy I knew in high school who looked like a mummy, you know, so we called him Cheops—it sounded like a funny nickname at the time."

None of them even forced a chuckle—especially not the one asking me the questions. He was all stone-like. I think he was the first detective at the scene. "Look, Mallory, we found you right there. You had the damned knife in your hand. How can you tell us that you didn't do it? Now, I want to know why you did it."

"Officer, I mean, Detective, I know how it looks, but honestly, I didn't kill the man."

Exasperated, he got up from his chair, and went over to pour himself a cup of what looked like mud from the ancient coffee maker, and then came back and stood over me, glancing up and down at my blood-splattered clothes. I thought he was going to offer me a cup, but then I realized differently. Not that I would've accepted it anyway. The stuff looked like something that had spilled out from a refinery.

"Mallory, is there a point you're trying to make about this guy's nickname?"

"Well, you asked me why," I said, clearing my throat.

"So why don't you tell us the reason then and cut out all the crap about the *Ten Commandments* movie."

I looked around the room at the faces staring at me. I could tell that, in their minds, I wasn't innocent until proven otherwise, I was already guilty. It was strange. I felt a sense of dread, but not about being held for homicide. It was for some other reason that I couldn't quite figure out.

"It wasn't Brynner's hairdo, you see. Everyone knows he's bald, but he was wearing this headdress that kind of hung down just above his shoulders and fanned out in ripples at the back of his head. Well, this black guy who worked across the street didn't have any headdress, but his hair was thick and combed down just above his shoulders, and it fanned out to the sides. It reminded me of Ramses' headdress blowing in the wind off the Nile. So, I nicknamed him the 'Pharaoh.'

11

I didn't know at the time that
I was right on target with the nickname"

The cold stares continued. Since I'm white and the guy I killed was black, they all probably thought that this thing was racially motivated—especially the large, black, cop with the hateful eyes who was standing at the back of the room. To him, I was probably no better than some Klansman, but wearing a shirt instead of the pointy-headed ghost costume.

He was Officer Baxter, and he addressed the detective who was questioning me, "Excuse me, Detective Puleio?"

Detective Puleio turned away from me to look back at the uniformed cop, "Yeah, Baxter, what is it?"

"This son of a—excuse me, this *suspect*, Mr. Mallory, has a previous history with us."

"Oh? And what is that?"

"I've been on the force for a while, and I researched and remembered this guy. Back in '92, after the King verdict in L.A. was announced, he was accused of assault and battery on an African-American man who was downtown peacefully protesting the verdict."

"He wasn't exactly *peacefully protesting!*" I cut in.

Detective Puleio turned and shot back at me, "Mr. Mallory, quiet, please, I want to hear this!" He turned back to Officer Baxter, "Okay, go on."

Baxter continued, "Well, the charges were eventually dropped because the D.A.'s office found *insufficient evidence* and figured we would lose at trial." He then turned those hateful eyes back at me again. "That's why this guy was still able to keep his job with the State."

I stared at Officer Baxter and said, "There's more to it, than what you're saying."

Detective Puleio turned back to me and held up his hand for silence. "For now, why don't you just tell us all about what happened today?" It was more a command than a request. He forced down another sip of the sludge from his coffee cup and sat in a chair. I avoided Officer Baxter's eyes as I looked around the room. I figured I'd better oblige Detective Puleio. No more nervous jokes about Cheops.

I'm a civil servant working for the State of New Jersey in Trenton. At least I was until this past week. Now, I don't think there's a union in the world that would represent me at a hearing to get my job back—no, not this time—even though I didn't kill the guy.

I worked in a position that the State deemed was necessary and worthy enough to spend New Jersey taxpayer dollars on to pay for my salary and benefits. It was nice to have the job. However, despite it being nice to have the job, I cannot with a straight face say that reviewing tax abatement applications from municipal governments to determine if an area is blighted and in need of rehabilitation is fabulously exciting work.

That being the case, one of the favorite ways to pass the time with my co-workers, at least those who would still associate with me after the incident that Officer Baxter referred to, was to look out the windows at the street below and the activity there. The commercial parking lot across from us is ten bucks for the entire day, not cheap for some of the salaries in this city. But if you buy a cup of coffee from one of the local merchants, you can get your ticket stamped for two hours of free parking. Maybe that's why the lot is so popular. It certainly seemed to keep the Pharaoh busy.

He was an attendant who handed out tickets when you entered the lot and collected your money when you exited. He wore these tortoise-shell shades, a green khaki uniform, and would comb his hair back, as I mentioned before. From the second-floor window, there didn't seem to be anything drastically unusual about him. However, one of my co-workers who occasionally parked there said that he was a real creep, and that he once gave her a hard time about how much money she owed.

About a week or so ago, I was standing at the window alone watching the lot, when I noticed that he put the cones out in front of the entrance—clearly a message that there were no more available spaces. Then he moved them to let certain customers enter. There must have been some spaces available. Why the favoritism?

Observing closer, it seemed that he lingered somewhat longer with these customers as they entered. He also seemed to be handing something over to them. Drugs? I couldn't tell. It didn't look as if any money was being exchanged. He didn't favor any one particular group. They were black, white, dressed professionally, or in blue-collar clothes.

There was something fishy about it. I thought that taking a closer look might be a fun way to extend my lunch hour by a few more minutes. It would make for good conversation around the office if anyone actually wanted to engage me in some.

The day after seeing this, two of my co-workers and I went for a walk after we finished our lunches. They sat in cubicles that were adjacent to mine. Because of what had

14

happened back in '92, I wasn't the most popular guy in our building, especially among our co-workers who weren't the same skin color as me. Arnie and Sam were two of the few exceptions who would still talk to me, and who would let me tag along on walks at lunchtime. Maybe they were giving me the benefit of the doubt because the charges against me had been dropped? Or, maybe it was just because sitting so close together and not talking would be awkward? I don't know. Whatever their reasons for including me, I was grateful.

Heading back to our office, I spotted the Pharaoh talking to a guy who, I assumed, had just parked his car in the lot. My curiosity at the window from the day before returned when I saw the Pharaoh press some piece of paper into the man's open palm.

Arnie and Sam were ready to cross the street to our building when I told them that I was kind of interested in what was going on at the parking lot booth. They both glanced at me rather apprehensively. I'm sure they were thinking about my past incident. Arnie suggested that maybe I shouldn't be staring at this total stranger, about whom I knew nothing, save that he combed his hair back above his shoulders.

But I was too curious. I told them to go on, that I'd be back to the office in a few minutes. Sam gave me a look, and an uneasy grin, which told me that this wasn't a good idea. But then he said, "Okay chief, suit yourself. We'll see you back at your desk with all the sordid details."

"Be careful, Don. Keep your distance," was what Arnie left me with as he turned to cross the street. I should have listened to him, but instead stepped a few paces closer.

15

I turned my attention away from them just in time to catch a glance at the face of the guy the Pharaoh was talking to. I was close enough to make out the words he said to the guy before the man went on his way.

He was white, maybe in his thirties, with a mustache and curly brown hair. He had a medium build and was dressed in light blue sports shirt and matching slacks. He looked normal, except for his eyes. They seemed frozen in place, as if preserved in ice beneath some wintry pond.

He looked as if he was in a trance, but he must have been coherent, because he was nodding his head as if to acknowledge that he knew what the Pharaoh was saying to him. I looked at his right fist. It was shaking from how hard he was clenching whatever the Pharaoh had given him. His frozen eyes had this stern look of determination in them. It was spooky.

But even spookier were the words I heard the Pharaoh utter to the mesmerized fellow before he hurried away to his destination: "Thou shalt do me great honor by delivering retribution upon my enemies, and restoring the vast treasures to my kingdom at Memphis—upon the shores of the great river."

Huh? Had I heard him right? This parking lot attendant wants this hypnotized, unquestioning lackey to punish someone and help rebuild his kingdom in Memphis, Tennessee, by the great river? What, the Mississippi River?

Had Elvis finally come back disguised as a black man working as a parking lot attendant in Trenton, New Jersey? I was on the verge of laughing, while watching this guy in his blue sports shirt and matching slacks dodge through traffic to the other side of the street. But something made me flinch, and I looked back at the Pharaoh.

He had turned and was now staring at me through his shades. "Hey, man, something wrong? What the hell're you lookin' at?" I hesitated, staring at him, and felt a flash of anger. Then I bolted from that side of the street. I could hear him laughing behind me.

When I got back, Arnie and Sam sensed something was wrong, but I told them that nothing had happened. I didn't know how to explain it to them. It wasn't just his words that had scared me. There was something else frightening about him. I wouldn't get up and look out the window the rest of that day.

The next day I came to work and, as usual, I went down to the cafeteria and picked up the local newspaper. There, on the front page, was the headline story about a tour guide who was murdered on the floor of the Trenton Museum. Apparently, he had been brutally stabbed several times, and his throat was slashed.

Normally, I paid no attention to these eye-popping stories and went immediately to the most important things—the comics. But this was different. People were talking about it all over my building. The Trenton Museum is about a four-block walk from our office. Arnie, Sam, and I occasionally stopped in there to look at the latest series of modern art and abstract paintings that none of us seemed to understand.

At first, the story only intrigued me. But once I got beyond the details of how the body had been found, and the personal matters about the victim (quiet guy, never missed a day of work, wife and three children, seven years with the Museum, etc.), it began to disturb me. There were two sentences, in particular, which were troublesome. They concerned the exhibit currently on display. It had been

17

publicized in the paper and we had even gotten a notice about it with our paychecks a few weeks ago. I had forgotten about it until now.

Five years ago, there was a discovery in Egypt of the second tomb of a Pharaoh whose prior tomb had been discovered years before. Apparently, this second crypt was a repository for many previously undiscovered treasures. Although this discovery was less publicized than the uncovering of Tutankhamun's tomb, it was more significant in the eyes of anthropologists because this crypt dated back to the years prior to 3000 B.C. King Tut's reign wasn't until after 1500 B.C.

As with many other states, New Jersey conducts a mass advertising blitz during summer to promote its tourism attractions. The current exhibit was going to tour the United States at a limited number of sites, a requirement of the Egyptian government. The various states and their museums had to convince the exhibitors that their locations would be the best. The exhibit could be a lift to the local economy, so New Jersey submitted its Museum in Trenton for consideration. Evidently, the Tourism Commission did a fantastic job in its presentation. Other major locations—such as Philadelphia's Museum, not far away—were passed up, and Trenton was chosen as one of the limited sites where the exhibit would be displayed. To the surprise of many, it became the first leg of the exhibit's national tour.

I began to sweat when I looked at the photo that appeared with the story. The caption underneath the picture read, "Police escort unidentified suspect away from scene of the killing. Witnesses say that he was found with a photograph of the victim, and a bloodied knife in his possession."

I let out a slight whimper as I looked at the face in the photo. He had stared right into the camera, with a cop escorting him at each arm. It was the unquestioning lackey from the previous day at the Pharaoh's booth. I recognized the hair, the moustache and, especially, the frozen stare in his eyes.

I live, or was living, in a one bedroom, one-bathroom apartment by myself. It's all I could afford after the divorce. She's the one who left me, but I still have to pay her alimony. It just doesn't seem right. At least we never had any kids; they would have cost me even more in the settlement. Even so, because we never had any kids, I feel like I lost something more anyway, something more than the money.

The apartment is in Ewing Township, one of the suburbs bordering Trenton. It wasn't much of a place for the rent that I paid, but it was a place to live, and at least it was outside of the city. It's a poorly-kept secret that no one employed by the State of New Jersey who works in Trenton actually wants to live there.

I had some dates here and there after she left me, but nothing ever took hold. Then, about a year or so ago, as I was approaching 50, I met Abby. It was the long Memorial Day weekend, and I decided to spend a few bucks on myself, and rent a place for a few days down at the Jersey Shore. I probably needed to save the money, but with my parents both gone, and no family in the area, I felt lonely and wanted to get away for a bit.

She was managing a breakfast place in Sea Isle City. Just a few years younger than me, she was divorced herself, with no kids, and doing okay financially. She saved her money well and had some good investments. It seemed like she was looking for someone to grow with her, and to grow old with her. When we first met, she was quite amused by my State worker jokes.

One night, several months ago, we were lying awake in bed at my apartment. Things had seemed to be growing a little distant between us, and I couldn't figure out why. When we would go places together, she just seemed to spend most of the time playing with her phone.

After laying in silence for a while, I got up the nerve to ask her, "Is anything wrong? Did I do something wrong?"

She looked at me, with raised eyebrows and asked, "Why would you ask that?"

"Oh, I don't know, you seem kind of . . . distant lately. Is there something on your mind that you want to talk about?"

She looked at me for a moment, as if deciding whether she wanted to talk. Then she laid her head back on the pillow, staring up at the ceiling fan doing its slow, circular dance. "Well, I've been thinking about my ex, and I'm trying to remember what it was about him that originally made me want to divorce him. Officially, it was over money problems, but that was probably not the main issue." She looked at me, waiting for a reaction. I stared back at her, not saying anything, wondering where this was going.

She asked, "What about you? We've never actually talked about your divorce, and why it happened. Did you leave your wife, or did she leave you?"

"It's not really something that I want to talk about."

But she pressed on, "Oh, come on now, please? I need to know more about you. We've been together for a while now, and I feel like I hardly know you. Come on, tell me about it."

I shook my head, and then let out a long breath, "If I tell you, will you tell me why you're divorced?"

"If I can remember."

I shook my head again. *Well, that's a convenient answer.* "Okay. We were married going on five years. She was working as a physical therapist in a hospital over in Pennsylvania."

"Which one?"

"Lower Bucks County, but that's not really important. The marriage started out well enough, but then we seemed to be growing apart. She wasn't happy with my job at the State. She felt like I should be starting my own business. I don't know—something like that.

"Well, after a while she became really friendly with another therapist at the hospital. You know, then one thing led to another and, eventually, one day she tells me that she's leaving to go live with this other guy, and she wants a divorce. No marriage counseling, no nothing."

Abby was laying on her side, her hand and elbow supporting her head, staring at me, with her ample breasts cascading over the top of the sheet. "What was the guy like? Did you ever meet him?"

"What do you mean, what was he like? Do you mean was he good-looking, did he have a nice build, what?"

She seemed frustrated, "You know, what was it about him that drew her to the guy?"

I heaved out a breath, shaking my head in frustration and remembrance.

"What, what was it about him?"

I looked at her, "He was . . . He was a black guy."

"Oh, I see." She stared at me for another moment.

"Are you going to tell me about your divorce now?"

She rolled over and pulled the sheet up over her shoulders. "Nope, it's not important now," and that was that. That was the last I would ever see of those ample breasts.

The next morning, I woke up just in time to see her gathering her toothbrush and the few other personal items that she kept at my place, as she was ready to walk out the door. When I sat on the edge of the bed to ask her why, she let out a sigh and said, "Look, Don, your ex-wife didn't leave you for that other guy because he was more handsome or had more money. And she didn't leave you because he was black, either."

Again, there was hesitation before she continued with a frustrated sigh, "She left you because your job and your life were just too dull. And now, you asked me last night what's bothering me lately. Well, now I realize that you're just too dull for me, too," and she closed the door with a slam.

I thought about running after her and saying to her that when you've got a previous history of being accused of assaulting someone, even though the charges were dropped, in this day and age, people will still find you guilty just because of suspicion. For that reason, you try to maintain a low, "dull" profile, so as not to bring any further, unwanted attention to yourself. But I stopped myself.

I had never told her about the arrest. She was still living in Sea Isle City, and never came to my office. The only reason for her to visit the Trenton area was for those times when she would stay over at my place. She really had no occasion to find out about this part of my past, and I wasn't going to bring it up now, so I didn't go after her. What was I going to do, try to bring up some fresh new State jokes about tax abatements to try and win her back? She was right. Beyond the government worker jokes, I was just being a dull and ordinary guy.

There were many nights since she'd left that I hadn't slept so well. That night, after seeing the photo of the unquestioning lackey, I didn't sleep well either, but it didn't have anything to do with missing Abby's warm body curled up next to me. Despite the bad night of sleep, I still got up at 5:30 the next day and went running. Even with being so tired, I covered my normal running course faster than usual.

That day was one of those days when the sun reminds us human beings of just how uncomfortable it can be, and that we just have to sit and take it. On days as hot as this, Arnie and Sam don't like to go for walks. They'll pass for the air-conditioned office, thank you. That worked fine for me. I wanted to walk to the Museum alone. Maybe I would find something at the exhibit to get rid of my fears about the Pharaoh.

I pounded the sidewalk the four blocks from my office building to the Museum. My feet and socks were going to stink from the sweat. It was better to occupy my mind with these thoughts about pungency, rather than what I might find.

The Museum was open again for business. The previous day, after the homicide, it had been closed and cordoned off for the police investigation. There was still a remnant of yellow crime scene tape attached to the double-handled doors, but it was obvious to the cops who the killer was, and they probably saw no reason to close the Museum just to spend several days scouring over the area.

As I mentioned earlier, this excavation didn't get as much media attention as King Tut's, so there were never throngs of curious people in attendance. Maybe people were disappointed because, as with the Tut Exhibit, there was no actual sarcophagus on display, or maybe it was because Boris Karloff was not standing there dressed as the Mummy, handing out autographs. But there were a few patrons in attendance. Some were probably there because they were more curious about the murder than the exhibit.

I drifted past the first few displays, glancing over the shoulders at the other customers who were viewing them. These were glass-encased descriptions of life in ancient Egypt and a chronicling of the excavation. They held no interest for me. Then I reached the photograph of the tomb, with its elaborate, sculpted head adorning the coffin. The headdress design was there. I thought again of Yul Brynner as Ramses in the movie. A supplementary photo, in black and white, showed the sarcophagus actually opened and the mummy lying in repose inside, the primitive wrappings enveloping him. The arms were also

24

individually wrapped, lying across one another on his chest. The face, or where it should have been, was completely covered in bandages. It was hardly Boris Karloff—hardly menacing.

But then I read the biography. His name was Menes (pronounced "meanies") and it stated that he was the King of Egypt from 3400 B.C. until an undetermined date. He was reputed to have founded a city on the Nile delta near Cairo. The name of that city is Memphis.

I rubbed clammy hands on my trousers as I again looked at the head sculpture in the photo. The picture never changed, but I saw him in it—the eyes, the headdress, the sealed lips. The golden figure of long dead Menes looked out at me from inside the framed photograph, but what I saw instead was the parking lot Pharaoh.

I backpedaled and bumped into another patron. Muttering something about being terribly sorry, I turned to run from the Museum. It was then that I noticed the security guard staring at me. He was probably in his fifties, graying in the moustache and the hair that peeked out from underneath the cap on his head. Through his glasses, I could see the way he looked at me. Even though the homicide investigation was over, the police had probably told security to keep an eye out for any suspicious individuals. Surely, I was the most suspicious-looking one at that moment.

Quickly, I turned from his stare. Feeling dizzy, I bumped into another patron coming through the Museum doors. At first, all I noticed was a tall, thin black man. *Another black guy*—another black guy, who would be mad at me just for accidentally bumping into him. However, when I attempted a forced apology, I got a quick glance at his face. He didn't speak a word, but his eyes said it all. They had the same soulless look as the servant whom the Pharaoh had sent to kill the tour guide.

He, too, carried something in his hand. I wasn't quite sure, but as he slipped it into the pocket of his khakis, it looked a lot like the back of a snapshot. I was out the door after that, not paying any more attention to the security guard or to the other employees that were staring at me.

It was him, Menes, the Great King of Egypt. I was convinced of it. He was here to punish those whom he thought had plundered his treasures and his sacred burial place.

As I hurried back to the office, people gave me odd stares. I felt ill at that moment, and I'm sure it showed. *How was I supposed to feel?* There was an Egyptian ghost sanctioning murders at the Trenton Museum. How was I going to make anyone believe that?

When they looked at my face, Arnie and Sam tried to lighten the mood. "Have you been eating those hot dogs from the street vendors again?"

"This is what happens when a guy like you tries to get culture."

Wisecrack comments aside, from the sickly way that I looked, both my co-workers and our office director agreed that I should take the rest of the day off.

At home that night, it was another bout of restless sleep, tossing and turning. I dreamt of venomous snakes striking out at faceless people who were trying to tear the stones from some pyramid. I remember waking up at one point wondering about what had happened to the archaeologists who had excavated the tomb.

26

I showed up at work the next day, unshaven and looking dreadful. There were looks of real concern from my co-workers. Things got worse when I saw the newspaper. The headlines were on fire again. There had been another murder at the Museum. The security guard who had looked at me with the intuitive eyes was dead, and the "alleged" killer had been caught with the dripping knife in his hand. It was the same drone I had stumbled into as I was fleeing the Museum. The eyes stared at me from the photograph in the paper. He was another unlikely suspect— good worker, family man. But he had become a killer, nonetheless.

I began to think about others I'd observed talking to the Pharaoh the weeks before. Had he recruited them also? Who had they murdered? Had a truck driver who delivered the exhibits to the Museum been killed? Maybe one of the Pharaoh's henchmen had made that death look like a traffic accident. Was there a vendor who provided trinkets to be sold at the exhibit murdered while walking down the sidewalk? Was that one made to look like a mugging? Would anyone ever make a connection to the Menes exhibit?

I spent that morning listlessly moving stacks of paper from one side of my desk to the other. Some, cynical of government employees, would call this a productive work day. My co-workers would come over to my cubicle and comment on how subdued I was.

"What's the matter, Don? Working for the State is not really that bad, is it?" Arnie joked.

I didn't laugh. "It's nothing." Then, from out of nowhere, I asked, "Arnie, do you know anything about scarab beetles?"

He raised his eyebrows. "Scarab beetles? I'm not sure what you mean."

"You know—scarab beetles. The Egyptians considered them sacred. Don't you ever watch the Discovery Channel?" I guess the question came out gruffly because he seemed to get this hurt look on his face.

"Don, are you alright? Is anything bothering you?" He was looking at me as if I needed a couple of vacation days at Trenton's Psychiatric Hospital. Many of my co-workers had given me the same look that morning.

"Just a little under the weather," I lied. He nodded and moved back toward his cubicle. Maybe he was just being polite, not wanting to pry. But I don't think that was it. I had a feeling he wanted to move even further away from me.

All morning I wrung my hands, wondering about which direction to take. Who would believe me? What could I do, go tell the police about my suspicions? I could just hear someone like Officer Baxter saying, *"Oh yeah, here's the white guy who we have a history with. Now he's accusing some parking lot attendant, who just happens to be black, of committing these murders. What's wrong with this picture?"*

This couldn't be happening. There must have been some small detail of reality I was overlooking. Mummies, or ghosts of mummies, just didn't come to life.

Slowly, I rose from my seat. My hands were sweating in my pockets as I walked over to the window. I looked out, and he was there. His hair was combed back, as usual. With the afternoon sun shining on it, his normally gray hair looked as golden as the sculpted headdress in the photograph at the Museum. He wasn't wearing his shades.

He was standing beside his booth looking up toward me. Our windows are tinted on the outside, but I just know he saw me right through the darkness. I sensed that he was challenging me. What would I do now, quit my job and run away?

No, my ex was gone, now Abby was gone, and many of my co-workers disliked me. I felt it was time for me to do something that would give me redemption from my feelings of guilt, something that would make all those people see me in a different light. I left for lunch early that day. There was a sporting goods store within walking distance. I was sure I could find what I needed there.

It was hot and very humid again, but I still wore my blazer out into the noonday sun. I would need it for concealment. The walk to the sporting goods store was disturbing. I looked at the faces around me. Any of them could have been one of Menes' drones sent to kill me as punishment for meddling with his vengeance. Some were laughing. I wondered if any of them knew what I knew. Any one of them could succumb to the will of the Pharaoh. How many had read about the murders? If they had read about them, how many knew, as I did, that this was one maniac who would never be caught?

The store was small and, at first, I was afraid they wouldn't have what I needed. But then I saw them in a glass case near the cash register. There was a decent selection to choose from. They ranged in size from small penknives and Swiss Army types, to a large, unwieldy Bowie. That one was a bit much for my needs. I found a handy fishing and camping knife, which would do just fine. It was the perfect thing for gutting bass, trout, or whatever happened to wash up along the Nile.

I didn't have enough cash on me, but they were happy to charge it. I hesitated somewhat when the salesman asked me if I wanted the sheath to go with it. I was thinking about how this purchase might look suspicious to the credit card company. I only use the credit cards for emergency purposes, or if I go out of town. "Sir?" It was the salesman—*another* black guy.

"What?"

"I asked if you wanted the sheath, sir. It's only five dollars more. It makes for easier carrying and accessibility when you're outdoors."

I knew that. I almost had a mind to tell the little, black twerp what I was really using it for. I didn't like the looks I kept getting from everyone lately. Security guards, my co-workers, people on the street, and even now from this, this...*guy*.

I was irritable and afraid. But I figured that I couldn't just stroll up to the Pharaoh with this shining dagger in my hand. It might help to conceal the knife by using the sheath and attaching it to my belt. I'd feel like a real desperado—like a mercenary.

"Yes, yes I'll take the sheath."

"Very good, sir. Would you like anything el -"

"No!No! Just ring up the stupid knife!" That drew few stares from some of the other customers and employees. Mr. Pushy Salesman was obviously taken aback.

"Yes...*sir!*" He wrung up my purchase with a sullen look on his face. I was drawing too much attention to myself. I had to get out of there.

Outside in the heat, I started having second thoughts. How could I go through with this plan? If I actually did it, the charge I made to my credit card would be the least of my worries.

But something overrode that concern. I couldn't let these murders continue. I wondered if I even had the guts to do it. But I had to try. Besides, I reasoned, once the deed was done, the police would see this creature for what he really was. Then they would have to believe me. That was it. It was not as if I were committing murder, because this guy was no human. This act was perfectly justified. This couldn't wait until night; the Pharaoh wouldn't be at the parking lot. I had to do it now, in the bright heat of the day, despite whatever might come of this.

I reached the parking lot and paused. There was an odd stillness in the air. The traffic, the sounds of the city around me, seemed to subside. It felt as if time had stopped, except for me. I looked to the left at my office building, the street reflecting off its windows. I imagined that no one was inside.

I became oblivious to the people on the street. They seemed to float by. The cars coming and going became more and more vague and hazy, until they were barely a blur on my periphery. My efforts were concentrated on reaching the Pharaoh's booth. I wouldn't be getting back to work from lunch. But that fact and all other concerns ceased, as my legs moved mechanically toward him. My hand slipped to the sheath concealed under my jacket. Unclipping it, I curled my fingers snugly around the knife handle. It felt warm and pliable in my palm.

Rapidly now, I approached the booth. Ten yards away—now eight, five, three. Suddenly, I realized it was empty. I started toward it, paused again, and then stepped inside. The heat was stifling. At first glance, I noticed

31

nothing out of the ordinary. There were parking passes, a time clock to stamp them, some napkins with what looked like smeared mustard, and a half-filled cup of soda, no ice.

But then I saw the photographs scattered on the back counter. I recognized the background in each picture. It was the Museum. One picture, in particular, struck me as familiar. It was a woman wearing a red blouse, maybe in her sixties, with thick glasses. She was an employee at the Museum who worked at the souvenir counter. I had caught a brief glimpse of her as I was fleeing the Museum that day. She was standing behind the counter, watching the commotion I had caused when I bumped into the assassin coming through the door. My glance at her could not have been more than two seconds, and I'm sure I never saw her other than that day at the Museum. But her image was printed in my head.

Sweat was pouring out of me. My foot bumped into something metallic. It was a waste basket underneath the counter. The only contents were four shreds of trash. They were two pictures torn in half. I reached down into the can and pulled the pieces out. I didn't even have to fit them together. One was the slaughtered tour guide, and the other was the suspicious security guard who had met the same end.

I guess all along I was hoping to find something to disprove this supernatural theory. But I knew then that I was right. The guard, the guide, the souvenir saleswoman—he meant to kill them all. These people didn't even have anything to do with the excavation. But his vengeful spirit did not discriminate. Apparently, anyone who was even remotely associated with stealing his

32

treasure was targeted. These were just employees of the Museum, but all of them were to be murdered.

I heard low laughter behind me. I wheeled around, and he was standing there in the entrance. My hand was already drawing the knife from the sheath. He stood there and raised a stumpy hand to show me the photo he was holding. It was my picture.

"Look Tut, or Menes, or whoever you are! I know all about you, and I'm going to kill you!"

His laughing stopped abruptly, and he looked grim. He dropped my photo from his hand. Suddenly, the shades popped from his face and fell to the floor. His eyes had bulged to about three times their normal size. They were no longer human. They looked reptilian.

Then his whole face changed. The cheekbones sank in, and pits appeared where his temples should have been. His gray, combed-back hair was spread out in the back, but suddenly fell to the ground in clumps. Within seconds it was gone, replaced by a great neck which fanned out at the sides, as a cobra's. His forehead was sinking in. The nose melted away until only his nostrils were barely visible at the tip. Eventually, the jaw shrank, becoming skinnier and more obtuse at the end. There were two fangs, one on either side. The only other teeth were the two larger, curving fangs which then protruded from the overlapping upper jaw. A forked tongue, oily black, flickered out between them. It was the head of some mutated snake, deadly poisonous.

The total transformation took only seconds. It took another second or two for the image to sink in, and then it lunged at me. I don't know how I did it, but I was able to dodge the lunging Pharaoh-cobra. At the same time, I slashed out with the knife, slicing through its throat. It staggered back, the blood spurting out in pulses that smacked against the glass panes of the booth. Right then I realized both arms had congealed into angry vipers themselves.

In a one-two motion, they leapt toward me. I ducked and slashed at each one successively, cutting lengthwise along their bellies. Blood erupted. I was speckled in some places and drenched in others. The creature fell backwards again. The body slid down the wall into a sitting position, its spasms causing more blood to gush forth.

I fell to my knees in front of the thing. I wanted to make sure the demon was cut out of the body. Gouging deeply again into the throat, I ripped the knife horizontally through the skin. Then I ripped again through each arm. Lastly, I worked on the chest. I needed to cut out his vengeful heart.

Then the appendages were shredded arms, not snakes. That didn't sink in until I had already sliced through many blood vessels. When I stood up I was looking down into the dead eyes of a mutilated parking lot attendant. It wasn't the Pharaoh anymore.

A shadow fell across the body. I dropped the knife and caught a glimpse of it hitting my bloody photo on the floor. I felt confused, rather than repulsed or amazed at what I had done. I looked around. The shadow belonged to a very large, black policeman who had his gun leveled squarely between my eyes. It was Officer Baxter.

Sitting in the police station now, knowing that he knew my past history, it's a wonder that he didn't just pull the trigger that day at the parking attendant's booth.

"So that's why I did it," I said to the incredulous cops staring at me in the Detective's Room. "You see, I didn't kill that parking lot attendant. I killed the Pharaoh. I liberated that evil spirit from his body. The Pharaoh is really the one who killed those guys."

"You son of a bitch!" Officer Baxter screamed, "You killed that guy in cold blood, just because he was a black man, and now you make up this supernatural crap to try and justify it! Rot in hell!"

"Officer Baxter!" Detective Puleio yelled back at him.

"You planted those pictures! You hired those people to murder the two victims in the Museum, and -."

"Officer Baxter!" Puleio yelled at him again. This time, Baxter stayed quiet. "Please leave the room. We are very calmly going to take the suspect and process him for homicide and arraignment. Now please go."

I blurted out, "Why would I hire a black guy to kill the Museum guard?"

Now Detective Puleio yelled at me, "Mr. Mallory, quiet, please! You've said enough!"

There were the hateful eyes of Officer Baxter upon me again. Then he turned and left the room in a flurry of cursing.

After that, they hauled me away to be fingerprinted and photographed, took my bloody clothes, replaced them with some gray prison garb, and locked me in a holding cell until the arraignment before a judge the next day. It should have been a traumatic experience for me. There was no remorse. Instead I felt more confused at what I had done than anything else. *How could I have been so swift and skillful at killing that thing?*

No bail had been set for me at the arraignment. An overworked public defender was assigned to my case. He just shook his head at my story. After I was arraigned, I was moved to the county jail a few days after the killing. They put me in a separate cell away from the rest of the population for my own safety. The brothers in here would surely hear about what I'd done to one of their own on the outside, and they wouldn't exactly be throwing a party to welcome me to the hood.

I had time to think. I thought about Abby, and what she would think of me now. *Maybe she would realize that being dull and ordinary isn't so bad after all.* There are worse alternatives.

Then I got a visit from Officer Baxter. I got scared because I thought he was going to come back and take out his own measure of justice. You hear stories about people getting arrested and then beaten up while they're in the holding cells. Baxter was a large man with a nightstick, a taser, and a gun, and he was quite capable of doing it.

Because he was a local cop that they all knew, the sheriff's deputies let him in my cell—something that was ordinarily not allowed except for the deputies themselves. I'm sure they figured that some runty white guy was not going to be able to overpower Baxter. If something should happen to me while Baxter was in there, they would believe him when he told them that I had just accidentally fallen, and someone would need to clean up the blood in my cell. He opened my cell door and came in, closing it behind him.

However, Officer Baxter did not appear menacing to me. As a matter of fact, he seemed to have a worried look on his face. I was sitting on the rock-hard cot. There was also a small chair in my cell. "Umm, Officer Baxter, you want to sit down?"

"No, I do not." His eyes were darting left and right across the cell. He was sweating.

He was nervous. That made me nervous. "Look, Officer Baxter, I know back at the police station you said that I had a history, but it's not like it seems. . ."

"Mallory, I don't want to hear about it now. Just listen . . ."

"Yeah, I might have said words to the guy, but he was mouthing off about the King verdict, and glaring at me as he walked past, and I swear he threw the first punch, but that's not what people saw . . ."

"Mallory, shut up! The guy was just on his way downtown to the protest, and you incited him. Don't tell me otherwise!"

I did shut up and, for a moment, Baxter's nervousness was gone and the old, hateful eyes were back. Then he shifted his eyes back and forth again, as if looking for something in the cell.

"Now listen to me, Mallory, and listen really good. Even though I'd like nothing better than to see you rot in here, or see something worse happen to you, there's something that I've got to tell you. The parking lot attendant you killed turned out to be a guy named Henry DuBois. No family to speak of—his parents were both dead, and he had no brothers or sisters. They were originally from New Orleans. They moved up north when Henry was still in his teens. He lived by himself in a small, shabby motel room off Brunswick Avenue that he paid off week to week."

It struck me that he said I had killed the man, instead of saying that I murdered him. "Officer Baxter—why are you telling me this?" I interrupted.

"Shut up, man! Just shut up and listen!" This was strange. He didn't look at all as if he wanted to mess me up.

Baxter looked outside the cell and down the hall. Seeing that no one else could hear him, he continued. "I got a friend down at the Coroner's Office. Your story seemed like such outrageous crap, but when my friend leaked this information to me, I figured I'd look into Henry's background."

"What did your friend tell you about Henry?"

"Man, shut up!" He leaned his face closer to me. "I'm getting to that. Just listen. It's important for you!" If I didn't know better, I'd say that he actually looked scared.

He continued, "It seems that DuBois and his folks were into black magic down there in Louisiana, and that Henry may have continued those hobbies. Some of his transient neighbors, who had lived for a while at that rat hole of a motel, said that the guy was scary. That was the reason none of them, including the desk clerk working at night, ever reported the screams they sometimes heard coming from Henry's room, like animals were being slaughtered in a pen. They were afraid of him."

I sat rigid on the cot. I could tell that Baxter didn't want to come out and say it was supernatural, but with Henry DuBois dabbling in such practices, we both knew it was. "Henry must have sympathized with the Pharaoh's grave being plundered, or maybe he owed some dark force a favor, and let the spirit use his body," Baxter continued.

We both stared at each other for a moment. "How did you know about DuBois?" Baxter asked.

"What do you mean?"

"How did you know what he was all about? How did you know he was into this black magic voodoo?"

"I didn't. I never knew Henry DuBois. I only knew about the Pharaoh in the parking lot—just like I told you cops."

Baxter leaned back away from me. He started backing up toward the cell door.

"Officer Baxter, are you going to tell me what your friend down at the Coroner's Office told you?"

He looked outside the cell again, and then around the inside, as if he was making sure no one else was in there. *Who else would be in the cell with us?*

Hesitatingly, Baxter said, "He said that on the knife you used they found something—something besides the blood."

"What? What did they find?"

"They found traces of some crude form of formaldehyde. The coroner couldn't believe it himself. He said it was like the kind the Egyptian medicine men had used to preserve their Pharaohs." Baxter practically whispered the last few words to me, shaking his head, trying not to believe.

It started coming to me. The Pharaoh had exiled his spirit from Henry's body, but he left something behind. It was the same stuff they used to mummify their beloved Pharaohs for preservation in the life hereafter.

Baxter had his hand on the cell door as he continued. His voice was shaky. "On a hunch, I went to the crime lab and sneaked a look at the lab report they're using as evidence against you. There were traces of the substance on the knife. You never heard it from me, but a good

39

lawyer might get you acquitted because the key piece of evidence seems to have been tampered with somehow. After all, *how else would the stuff get on there?* It's a technicality, and a long shot, but it just might get you off."

I jumped up from the cot. "Baxter! Baxter, you've got to help me!"

He came forward, pushing me back down. "NO!" he shouted. He looked out of the cell. Some of the deputies down the hall looked up. He gave them a quick, nervous smile, as if everything was okay. They went back to their work.

He turned back to me and whispered fiercely, "I ain't testifying. Man, I never want to see your face again or cross your path! If you get out, just get away from here, get away as fast as you can. I think you know why!"

No, I didn't. "Know what? What am I supposed to know?"

As he quickly slid the door open, the last thing he told me was that I was like the Plague to him. I jumped up again from the cot and grabbed the bars of the cell door just as he slammed it shut. "Baxter! Officer Baxter! You've got to help me!" But he kept moving down the hall, never looking back.

It was yesterday that Officer Baxter came to see me. I didn't understand his last words, and his revulsion at being around me. But it has started sinking in over these last few hours.

Remember how I felt confused rather than sickened over what I'd done? Maybe it was the same for the others that the Pharaoh had used. You see, all this time I thought I was the one in control. I thought that I had come up with this plan to kill the Pharaoh and save the streets from a murderous creature. But it wasn't me. He was in control the whole time, from the moment I laid eyes on him as Henry DuBois in that parking lot.

Menes was too clever for me. He knew that the police would eventually be led to Henry, probably by me. They'd find the torn-up photos of the Museum victims and put it all together. But having the parking lot attendant murdered was the perfect way to set me up. Instead of Henry being accused, the cops found me standing over him with a dripping knife. That's right, me, the guy who had a history from back in '92 of assaulting another black man, me, the guy who they thought should have been convicted back then.

I also know why Officer Baxter was so afraid of me. I know why he ran, and why he told me to get far away, but that won't do any good. Getting freed is just what the Pharaoh wants for me. Officer Baxter had said the technicality would be a long shot toward getting me acquitted, but I don't think so. After all, they couldn't charge me the last time either. It will be easy. Everything is easy for the master to arrange.

You see, the cops were right. I did kill Henry DuBois after all. I thought that by doing so, I would exorcise the Pharaoh's spirit, but I was wrong. I was deceived.

It's floating out there, waiting for the right moment. He's still not finished, and he needs a vehicle with which to carry on. He liked what I did to Henry. Who would be better at this mayhem than me, a man once thought to be dull, but with enough hatred inside to want to kill someone? Who best to continue the carnage than me, someone who still carries a grudge, just like the Pharaoh, and who is looking for revenge for having been wronged?

A moment ago, I heard a soft wind blowing down the cell corridor. It's getting louder and picking up speed, coming closer from another land – from another time. It's the master coming. He has a task for me.

In the desert, they call this wind a sirocco. It's blowing in from off the Nile, carrying with it a smell. There's the stench of a thousand rotting scarab beetles, whiffs of ancient burial rites and decrepit tombs . . . A stench of death, more death.

I originally sent this story to a cool magazine called **The First Line.** *It's a quarterly, and the concept is that for each quarter of the year, they create a first line, and then you build your own story from there and send it in. They then get a plethora of stories with various takes on that first line. I actually got a personal, emailed response on this one from them, as opposed to the usual canned rejections. They liked the story, well-written, they said, but had some issues with confusing points of view and other matters. They encouraged me to give them another try. Ah, but one gets so busy with raising a family, and the demands of a government job, so I never got around to sending them another story. You get this one instead, cleaned up from my first attempt. Consider this my contribution to the feminist movement. Knock 'em dead, ladies.*

THEIR TURN

It was the holidays, and Mary knew, especially during this season, that it would be dangerous to try and cross her husband. She had learned about his anger at their first anniversary. With brute force he had made it clear to her that she was to serve him without complaint. The holidays were *his* time for feasting and revelry, and for choosing a new bride. Yet, regardless of the peril she might face, she also knew that now was the time for her and the others to act.

She watched from the shadows as Chloe was forced to celebrate her own first anniversary by helping their husband, Jackson Remington Leedsworth, prepare for his festivities. He sat at the table in his study, its hand-carved elegance symbolic of the way he portrayed himself outside the walls of the antebellum mansion where the wives were imprisoned. After Chloe finished brushing his gray, shoulder length hair, she smoothed out the wrinkles of his formal coat—her snowy, white fingers contrasting its blackness. It had been packed away since he had worn it a year ago.

Chloe asked him, "Is everything to your liking, my lord?" With barely a smile of appreciation he grunted at her that it was.

Mary might have seethed with anger at the way Chloe was forced to fawn over him. But giving way to wrath would expose her. He did not tolerate dissonance in his home, and the consequences of spying would be grave. She had to control her instincts.

She thought back to that night eight years ago. "J.R.," as he was affectionately known in certain circles of Savannah, had a way when courting a lady; so many of them had found his genteel drawl and other charms too much to resist. However, once back at the mansion, the proper Southern gentleman ruled with a disciplined tyranny. Mary had asked, "But I do not understand, my lord, when we first met, you said that you wanted me to be your own. Why then did you bring me here? Why did you take me as your bride if there were others?"

He had commanded her to be silent. "Your duty is to serve me. None have ever disobeyed, and neither shall you."

Still she persisted, "But what about my needs, my desire?" With that, he cut her pleading short by clenching his fingers around her milky throat. She had learned a lesson. His will and brutality had taught her to at least *show* fealty to him.

However, from that point on, she had plotted for this night. Conditioning herself not to expose her thoughts, she would only contemplate her treason when he was otherwise occupied. It actually helped that he showed no use or concern for her. This enabled her to stay out of his sight most of the time.

The moon was high. Jackson rose from the table. With his pampering complete, he was ready to seek out another bride. Although the holidays were miserable for his wives, Jackson relished them.

Chloe had groomed him well. She looked up at their master. Mary noticed that he regarded Chloe almost thoughtfully. "You have served me well, my wife. You know your place." In a rare moment of tenderness, he reached out and caressed her cheek with his nails. Mary twitched, hiding behind a column. She remembered that same gesture from their first night together. At the time, it seemed to her the caress of a gentle giant. If only he had kept his promise to love and cherish, to always satisfy her hunger and thirst.

Suddenly, she felt him inside her mind. The thoughts of their first night together had caused her to let down her guard only for a moment, but it was enough. He could feel her presence behind the column. Things would happen quickly now.

Mary knew that his palm was rough as a mongrel's paw. Still, Chloe tilted her head lightly against it. "I am at your service always, my lord," she sighed. He smiled slightly, not revealing his teeth. Mary felt him in her mind, revealing that he would deal with her severely before he left. She was delaying his hunt. He gently commanded Chloe, "Go now, young one, wait with the others. That is your place now." Obediently, with no hint of emotion, Chloe turned and glided away into the musty shadows.

He turned now to face Mary, who had emerged from behind the column. She stared boldly at him. She thrust into his mind; *give me all your rage*. He hissed at her, "Your spying and insolence will bring you agony! Never again will you affront me!"

He lunged at her, but stopped in mid-flight when he saw the red, soulless eyes all open at the same time, blazing at him from the shadows, more than a hundred pairs of them. From the swirling darkness of his study, the other wives that Jackson had wed in unholy matrimony converged behind Mary.

He knew that, had they been alive, even his sprawling mansion could not have housed them all. Now, as undead spirits, only materializing into physical form when necessary, what need did they have for physical space? Indeed, if not for Jackson's supernatural will upon them, none would be confined to his elegant prison.

Depending upon which era they had been taken from, the image of what was once clothing was different among them. Some wore Victorian dresses. These were the matronly women from the Georgia of many years past. Others were clad in designer sweaters and spandex pants from the 80s, styles that had filtered down from expensive Yankee stores in New York and Boston. Finally, there were those dressed as Mary, professional women by day, club hoppers at night. They represented the new South, with its chic Atlanta, and retro riverboat gambling in Biloxi. Jackson had watched closely as the styles had changed through the years. He had been a vampire for a long time. As Mary and the others had learned, style was important to him. No girls from a textile mill—thank you. After all, he fashioned himself a gentleman.

Mary knew that the gentleman vampire loathed the behavior of others of his kind—those uncouth gluttons who gorged themselves on both animals and common mortals.

47

He believed in moderation, and selectivity, and that a feast should be savored, not consumed, as if it were simply a T.V. dinner.

For most of the earthly year, he kept a leash on his appetite and refrained from dining and drinking. But during the holidays, when mortals celebrated, and females dressed magnificently for the festivities, even he, an aristocratic creature of the night, would give in to the same vulgar lust that drove his barbaric brethren. Ultimately, what mattered most was the fluid, flowing dark and luscious, like a sanguine delta river, beneath perfumed flesh.

Even now, as they slowly moved toward him, they looked elegant, despite the pallor of the grave hanging over each undead face. Mary realized that he was taken in by their grace and had let down his own guard. He bellowed, "Get back, all of you! Your punishment will be long and severe!" But his vulnerability was apparent. His face was like a whole pack of wolves on the prowl combined into one visage, yet the brides saw a glimpse of fear there for the first time. He drew back his jaw, exposing deadly canines, but his mouth was more a grimace than a snarl, and his sophisticated voice quivered.

There were some, those from the Civil War and Reconstruction era, who were more proper than others. In life, they had been instructed to be submissive to their men, to obey commands without question, and this had carried over into their unnatural death when Jackson had taken them. It had taken Mary to convince them over these eight years to change that belief. In life, Mary had been a woman with modern liberations, who no longer served a man without question. She had her own ideas of how to run her life—and her supernatural death.

For decade upon decade they had hungered, their master never even allowing them a naïve schoolboy to feast upon. Mary had provided them the opportunity. Now their fangs grew longer in anticipation.

"I said get back!" but he could not control them all. He was backing up. Mary knew that he could bend the will of several, but not great numbers of them at the same time. Suddenly, she felt Jackson focus his wrath back on her. He knew she was the one who had caused this treason. If he destroyed her, the rest would cower back.

He sent daggers into her undead mind, causing her spirited form to ripple in pain, as if crumpling over. "Yes, you are mine now, and you will pay dearly for your transgressions against . . ."

The words died in his mouth, as a wooden stake plunged through his back and burst through his chest. His demonic heart, glowing molten-like and misshapen, dangled, and then dripped, from the sharp point. His screams shook the columns of the mansion. When he turned, his body gave out and crumpled. As he burst into flames, he saw Chloe standing over him, sharp teeth gleaming against wine-colored lips.

Chloe, the youngest of them all, was the one that Mary had convinced to do the actual deed. Mary rose back up from the mist of the floor and watched. At Chloe's feet, Jackson's ashes gathered in clumps like the Spanish moss clinging to the trees outside. He had been killed with a commoner's weapon, something that a girl who worked in a textile mill might use. There was nothing genteel about the second and final death of Jackson Remington Leedsworth.

Chloe's pleasure in killing their master was obvious. Jackson had concentrated his fury so intently on Mary that he had lost track of his newest bride, the most jealous of them all. In life, Chloe had completed the change in women. For her own part, Mary knew that she was merely cunning by not playing the dutiful wife. On the other hand, she knew that Chloe was the ultimate modern woman, young, jealous, and impetuous enough to agree to destroy an undead tyrant.

The others gathered around Mary, so grateful to her. One of them shrieked, "All pay homage to Mary, our new Queen!" They knelt down before her. The last to do so was Chloe. Her glowing red eyes met Mary's just for a moment. Then she bowed down her head, grinning through a mouthful of jagged blades. Mary regarded the impetuous one and thought to herself, *Queen, yes, but I will have to watch my back.*

At least for now, though, there would be no further treason. The holiday festivities, and the true home of these brides of darkness, the intoxicating night, beckoned to them. Blood-filled, robust men were out on the town, so many fangs tingled at the thought. After hungering and thirsting through the decades, finally, it was their turn.

Most of the people who live in Florida, and definitely those in Citra, in Marion County, then east, and then north through the towns in Bradford County, know Route 301. As noted in the story, it's a connecting Route from Interstate 75 to Interstate 10 in the northeast part of the State. Such residents will also recognize the actual towns that I gave fictitious names to. This story could have taken place in any one of those towns, but I chose "Staunche" as the main setting because of the particular feeling I get when we travel back and forth through it. Though we've passed through it many times, I should note that we've never actually stopped to check out the town. Unlike the residents in this story, I'm sure the actual residents are very friendly and accommodating. At least, I'm pretty sure they are.

ROUTE 301

"It looks like you folks are heading through Staunche to get to where you're going, did I get that about right?" the American Gas station attendant asked. Rick Russo was walking around to the passenger side of the car as the man was talking to him. The attendant had just finished filling the tank and checking the oil of the Russo's Acura. Unlike in New Jersey, in most places in the South Rick had to pump his own gas, so he was pleasantly surprised that this rare, old-fashioned service still existed in some places down here. He thought, *I guess that's just how they do it here in Wendell.* He and Janine had snickered at the name of the town when they pulled in to fuel up. To them, it was just another one of those hayseed backwaters of Florida that one passes through on the way to the more touristy destinations. The name "Wendell" seemed to fit their impression of the small town.

But now the guy was taking too long, looking back and forth at the car, and through the wind shield at him and Janine. Rick had gotten impatient waiting for him to come around to the driver's side for payment. Besides, being an English teacher, it struck Rick that the guy should have separated the declarative from the interrogatory as two different sentences, but instead he had combined them into one bad run-on. *Now that was annoying.*

Rick stared at the man wearing the dirty cap with the green dinosaur symbol on it, thinking that the guy was so old that he looked like he was from the age of dinosaurs, himself. If this town was a hayseed backwater, then this guy must be the resident huckleberry.

Not wanting to bother the man with using his credit card, Rick pulled $40 in cash from his wallet and handed it over. "Keep the change. We *are* going to I-10; don't we have to go through Staunche to get there?"

The old man took the two 20s and put them in his shirt pocket, "Much obliged, sir, thank you." He looked away for a moment and then asked, "Y'all came up from somewhere down off 75 and took 301 as a shortcut, tell me is that right?"

Hmm . . . Another bad run-on sentence, sheer genius, Rick thought. "Well, as a matter of fact that's correct. We were down in Naples for a week and thought on the way home we'd spend a day or two in Savannah. I've got to get to Interstate 10 to get back on 95 and into Savannah, right?" Rick was getting more annoyed with the questions; he just wanted to get back on the road. It was only early summer, but already plenty hot at 10 in the morning, and he wasn't interested in making small talk with the locals, at least not here in Wendell, anyway. It had been a long ride up from Naples, and they still had about three hours of traveling to get into Savannah. The stopover would do them good before the long drive back to New Jersey.

"Hey babe, is everything alright?" Janine had put down her phone and was looking out the passenger window, watching through her designer shades.

Rick turned to her briefly, "Yes, everything's fine," and then looked back at the attendant.

The old man ignored her. "Not that I mind the business, mind you, but y'all would have been better off just driving the extra miles and picking up 10 off 75. That's all I'm saying."

"Oh, and why is that? Someone in Naples suggested that on the way home we take 301 instead as a shortcut."

The attendant squinted into the warming sun, seeming like he was pondering something. "Well, it's just that the State Prison is in Staunche. Did you know that? The folks who live down in Naples who told you to go this way probably don't know nothing about that."

Rick wasn't aware of that. "So what? Even if those people in Naples didn't know *nothing* about it, why is that a problem? Have the prisoners escaped and begun running amok all over Route 301?"

The old man got in close to Rick's face and said, "No mister, it ain't because the prisoners are running around. It's because the people in Staunche ain't right, that's all. That's why they put the prison there."

"What are you talking about, they *ain't* right?" Rick sneered.

The attendant sighed. "Look, you folks are down here on vacation from up north, right? It's just that the people in Staunche believe that you can't get something for nothing."

Rick shook his head, as the old man continued. "The people in Staunche know, according to which way

54

y'all are going, you're using 301 to get through their town to either vacation up north on 95 or further down south in Florida. For the privilege of you driving through their town and enjoying the leisure that they'll probably never know, you've got to give something up." He paused and then said, "You've got to leave something behind."

Rick burst out laughing. Clearly, the old man was offended by that. His leathery face scrunched up as if he had just bitten into something rotten.

"Rick, can we get going now?" Janine made no attempt to hide the annoyance that was both in her voice, and on her face with its high cheek bones.

"Yes, yes, we're going." He shook his head at the attendant and headed around to the driver's side, slamming the door as he got in. He was startled when he realized the guy had followed him around and now peered through the open window.

"I'm just warning you, mister, you and your lady, y'all just keep going through Staunche. Don't stop to eat or go sightseeing or nothing like that. Y'all just keep going till you get yourself onto I-10."

Rick turned the ignition and gunned the engine, visibly annoyed. He smirked at the attendant, "Oh *we'all* will be sure to do that, Jasper. Don't worry your simple head. *"Sightseeing in Staunche*—unbelievable!"

Janine looked past Rick at the attendant and added with a caustic smile, "Have a nice day!" The old man pulled his hands off the door just as Rick pulled away and screeched back north onto Route 301, not looking for oncoming traffic.

The attendant stared at the back of the car as it spun down the road. He shook his head, muttering to himself,

"Snooty bastards and their Jap car. Try to do them a favor and give some sound advice, and they just go on their merry little way. Lord, help them."

Rick slowed down once they were out of sight of the gas station. He remembered warnings that he had received from other vacationers to obey the speed limit through these towns. He and Janine were both silent in the car for a moment. Then they looked at each other and grinned. Rick rolled his eyes. "*Wendell!* It won't be too long before we're traveling through there again!" he said. They both started laughing, knowing that was never going to happen.

Janine continued snickering. "What were you and that old yahoo talking about anyway?"

"I tried to correct him on his poor use of grammar, and he didn't like it," he kidded her.

"Oh, I don't doubt that." Being an English teacher herself, and knowing how meticulous he was about sentence structure, she would only half-believe that he was kidding. Cut from the same fabric as him, she also got annoyed at the frequent butchering of the language.

Rick had met her when they began teaching at the same public high school in an affluent suburb in Somerset County, New Jersey, after having been hired at about the same time five years earlier. He liked her reputation among the other faculty and the students, of being very demanding—just as he was. They each loved the language, and were appalled at the dismal state that grammar had fallen into—especially among students, high school and otherwise.

56

The fact that she was very attractive didn't hurt either. Rick knew that any sophomore male who may have secretly dreamed of the strawberry blonde hair and hazel eyes that crowned Janine's shapely figure, soon had such dreams shattered when he realized that she wouldn't take any crap, and actually expected them to get their homework done, even if they were a star on the basketball team. He was always amused by the fact that she wasn't afraid to use sarcasm to put down such a student. Very effective as teachers, their methods were rarely challenged.

Smiling now as he drove, Rick thought about how it was inevitable that they had eventually gotten together. They amused themselves by trying to outdo each other in planning their lessons. He shook his head, thinking and chuckling about the time an actual argument broke out between them as to who was the better grammarian, William Strunk or E. B. White.

"What's so funny, babe?" she asked.

"Oh nothing, Ms. Smith, just thinking about how great it is to be married to you." She grinned. Rick always knew that she would never take his last name. Smith was so much more of a stern name for a teacher, a name that was to the point, just like the person who bore it.

Life felt good to him this summer, and he was sure it felt good to her, too. They had no kids of their own (they only wanted to teach them, not raise them), had two good salaries with benefits, the Acura, and the Land Rover back at their home with the two-car garage. Now they were spending two weeks driving down and back to Florida, staying in pleasant hotels, eating spicy, southern food, and quaffing many rum-soaked drinks. With all that, why be bothered by thoughts of the old attendant back at the gas station?

They rode in silence for a few more minutes, Janine going back to her phone. Rick then started hitting the seek button on the radio. "Listen to all this crap. There's nothing but gospel and country. What're the chances the people around here play some Mozart?" He had something new to be annoyed about.

"Why don't you just put on a CD—or something off your phone," Janine said. "You know, it's really annoying the way you keep playing with the radio." He ignored her and tried one of the presets again. She looked away at the roadside gliding by, and saw the sign noting that Staunche was five miles ahead.

Finished fiddling with the radio, Rick had also noticed the sign for Staunche. He pressed the CD button. A symphonic version of some heavy metal song came on. "The old geezer back there told me that we shouldn't stop for anything in Staunche. He said there's a state prison there."

"So?" Janine asked, "Is the whole town a state prison? What, are no civilians allowed to walk around the town?"

He chuckled slightly, "Yes, that's kind of what I said to him."

"And how did he respond?"

"Oh, I don't think he liked it too much. He said something about the people in Staunche 'just ain't right.' He said some kind of craziness about them wanting something out of you for the privilege of driving through their town on the way to your vacation."

Janine laughed out loud. "Oh, babe, that sounds just like something out of *Deliverance*. That guy's probably been drinking anti-freeze back in that garage." He laughed at that thought.

Between her playing with the phone and the two of them laughing, neither noticed the "Staunche Town Limits" sign, nor the speed limit signs that dropped to 55, and seconds later, to 45. The speed trap was behind a tattered billboard right after the 45 MPH sign. Rick was doing 60 when he passed the police cruiser. A few seconds later, he saw the flashing blue lights in his rearview mirror.

"Oh for...I can't believe it! Now I'm going to get a speeding ticket from Barney Fife!" Rick shook his head in exasperation as he pulled over to the shoulder.

Janine berated him, "Why weren't you paying attention? How could you let this happen?"

"Janine, will you just lay off me, huh?"

She collected herself for a moment. "Alright, alright, let's just calm down. Be polite. Maybe he'll let us off with a warning."

Rick smirked, "Yeah, fat chance of that. Can you get the insurance and registration out of the glove compartment?"

The officer first walked up on the passenger side, glanced in at a forcefully-smiling Janine, went back around the car, seeming to study the New Jersey license plate, and then came up to the driver's side window, which Rick had already rolled down.

"Good morning, officer," Rick tried to keep an even keel to his voice.

"Good morning, sir. License and registration, please," he said—peering into the window. The nametag said Patrolman A. Wertz. He smiled through very good-looking teeth. Rick saw his own nervous expression in the reflection of the officer's sunglasses. Patrolman A. Wertz had a strong build, a good-looking man. Rick knew right away that he wasn't dealing with Barney Fife.

Patrolman Wertz finished looking over Rick's license and registration and handed it back to him. Janine still held the insurance card in her hands. The officer hadn't asked for it. "Mr. Russo, do you know why I stopped you, sir?" He had the usual southern accent, but spoke very good English. *Maybe I should complement him on that*, Rick thought to himself. *Maybe then he will give us a warning.*

"I'm not sure, was I speeding?" He smiled nervously.

"Yes, sir, I clocked you at 60 in a 45 mile per hour zone. We strictly enforce the speed limit here in Staunche." He smiled back at Rick, but not sarcastically.

"Really, are we in Staunche already?" Rick looked genuinely surprised.

Officer Wertz's expression turned serious. "Do you mean to tell me you weren't paying attention while you were driving, sir?"Rick felt the hard look from Wertz's eyes despite not being able to see them through the sunglasses. He actually gulped.

Janine leapt in, smiling, leaning across Rick. "Oh, we're sorry, Officer. We've just been having such a wonderful time in your great State of Florida. We were laughing about all the good times and must have missed the change in speed limit. We're sorry."

Patrolman Wertz removed his sunglasses, stony eyes staring at her for a moment, and then seemed to relax.

His professional smile returned, as he replaced his shades. He put both hands on the door and leaned in. "Well, you two look like some nice folks from New Jersey. I'm going to let you go with a warning. Just be careful driving and enjoy your time here. We strictly enforce the speed limit here in Staunche."

"Yes, you told us that al-," and Rick caught himself. "Thank you, thank you kindly, Officer." He realized how stupid his and Janine's smiles must have looked. But Patrolman Wertz let it go. "Have you folks eaten anything yet this fine morning?" he asked.

"I'm sorry?" Rick responded.

"If you're hungry, there's a great place right here in town, called 'Granny's Ham 'N Hash Diner.' Best darn pie you'll ever taste. You should stop in and have a bite. Take a little break from the road and see about our nice, little town here."

"Well, I am a little hungry. Maybe we will do that. Thanks again, Officer," Rick said. Janine leaned over again and gave Patrolman Wertz her best cheery face.

"You folks have a good day now." He backed away and walked to his cruiser.

Rick and Janine looked at each other and gave a collective breath of relief. Fortunately for them, there was no traffic coming at that moment, because Rick again pulled out, slowly this time, without looking in his rearview mirror. Neither of them saw Patrolman Wertz leaning against the cruiser, studying their car and talking on his radio as they drove off.

As with the other towns they had gone through on Route 301, Lawton, and Wendell, the highway essentially became Main Street as it made its way through Staunche.

Rick kept it at a respectable 25 miles per hour. They both took in the sights, the silence slightly uncomfortable between them. There were gas stations on either side of the road, a dollar store, and a Piggly Wiggly grocery store.

Just past the First Baptist Church on the left, they saw a storefront that said "Guns, Fireworks, and Jewelry." They both laughed again. Rick shook his head, "Unbelievable. Classic redneck style."

Janine held up her arm, showing her watch and, in a mocking, southern accent said, "You see this here wristwatch? This here fine timepiece is both a clock and a Glock." Rick laughed.

Another half mile up and the road passed over a stream. The sign read, "Alligator Creek." Janine said, "That must be where they dump the bodies." Rick nodded and grinned.

They were both relaxed again, shaking off the encounter with the police officer. Then Janine saw it, down on the next corner of Main and Call Streets. It was the "Ham 'N Hash Diner." "Hey babe, there's the diner that cop was talking about."

"Yes, so what?" Rick asked.

"Well, we only stopped for that quick bagel near Ocala. I am still a little hungry. Why don't we stop and get a little something else to eat?"

Rick glanced over and chided her, "Oh, I don't know. That old yahoo back at the gas station said we shouldn't stop for anything in Staunche. The prisoners might get us, you know."

"Oh, come on. I could use a little break from the road, anyway."

He sighed, "Yes, okay, I guess we could use a little break." He turned left at the light and pulled into the Diner's parking lot.

They seated themselves at a small booth by a window. The table had one of those mini jukeboxes. It reminded Rick of the old diners in New Jersey. Thumbing through the selections, he said, "Look at these songs: 'Peggy Sue,' 'Rock Around the Clock,' 'Smoke Gets in Your Eyes.' Like a regular '50s revival."

Janine asked, "Do you think they have '50s prices to match?" She paused while looking at the menu, "Well, not exactly, but not bad either." The countertops, the mirrors reflecting the soda fountains, and the flat, swiveling counter stools with their robin's egg blue color had an old-fashioned look to them, but the waitress who was now coming to take their order did not.

She was wearing a pastel orange uniform. Her nametag said "Amber," but her hair certainly wasn't. It was dark, but shot through with random strands that were purple, green, and orange, like the colors of an oil slick on water. It was as if one of her high school friends had done a bad job of trying to highlight it for her. The small, bone earring embedded above her left eyebrow completed her fashion statement. Janine could barely restrain from shaking her head as the girl stopped by their table.

"Hi, folks, how y'all doin'?"

"Oh, we're doin' just fine," Janine replied, stifling a snicker. "What do you recommend?"

"Well, the chili's great, and you can never go wrong with a club sandwich. But y'all just have to save room for some of Granny's pecan pie. It's to die for."

Rick was looking at her lipstick, which was on so thick that it stained her teeth. She was probably a local girl who had started working in the Diner right out of high school. He guessed that she probably had some white trash boyfriend, maybe working in a garage somewhere, whom she would marry, get fat with, and become wrinkled with at too early an age, due to them both chain smoking. *They'll probably spawn a litter of chubby kids along the way, too. She won't ever know anything better than this life.*

"I don't know," Rick said, "I'm not sure that I want a whole meal. What do you think, babe?"

Amber turned her lipstick-stained teeth toward Janine. Janine paused a minute, "Hmm . . . I guess we can just go with a piece of that pie. Are you *sure* it's really the best?"

If Amber detected a hint of mockery, she didn't let on. "No better pie in all the South, ma'am. Grandma Tina, the proprietor here, we all call her Granny, she makes them all by herself. Some folks say it's more like she casts a magic spell over that pie, instead of baking it from a secret recipe. We all call her Granny Tina, but her real name's 'U-tina.' It's Indian. Oops, wait a minute, I mean Native 'merican, sorry. Her own granny was full-blooded Timucuan but married a white man. She says her name got angle-sized through the years. Her name means 'Woman of my Country.' Ain't that sweet?"

"My, my, that's quite the history lesson considering it's about a piece of pie," Janine said.

"Yes ma'am. If you find a better-tasting pie, the head cook here will probably step out in front of a semi coming down Route 301 out there, 'cause he'll be so let down. Even though he doesn't bake 'em himself, he's so proud to serve Granny's pie here." She guffawed at her own joke, a sound like a braying mule.

Janine smiled back at her. "Sounds good, I'll take a slice."

Rick was musing to himself that the girl had actually known how to correctly pronounce a word like proprietor, but not Anglicized. "Make it two," he finally chimed in, just a hint of patronizing in his voice. "I think we can each have our own piece."

"If you don't finish, y'all can take it with you for later. It keeps real good, even in the heat of the day. Y'all want some ice cream on top of that?"

"No," Rick said, "not at 11:00 in the morning. I'm sure Granny's *special* pie will be plenty enough without her *special* ice cream."

Amber scribbled their order on her pad. "Alrighty then, it's coming right up." As she turned, they both snickered, watching her ample, pastel-colored rear end waddling toward the kitchen. Neither of them noticed the dark face of the cook who had come out the opposite kitchen door and was watching them from behind the counter. He ducked back inside before they looked his way.

The two English teachers grinned at each other. "Granny's pie," Janine said. "You think Granny's actually back there baking them daily?"

"And whose Granny is it anyway?" Rick asked. He looked around again. There were about a dozen people in the Diner, none really paying too much attention to them, even though these people could probably tell that the two of them were not from Staunche, Wendell, Lawton, or Bailiwick, or anywhere else up or down Route 301. It was a weekday, so they were primarily older, maybe retired folks.

They had bespectacled faces with gray hair and age lines that were as long and deep as the South and its culture. Rick and Janine listened to the quiet conversations going on around them, drinking in the southern drawls that eased from the tongues.

Perky Amber was coming back with their pieces of pie. Both were stacked with huge scoops of vanilla ice cream. "Here you go, folks, enjoy! Can I get y'all anything else?"

"Uh, you could start by getting the order right," Janine said.

Amber gave her a puzzled look. "Anything wrong, ma'am?"

Janine shook her head, "Well, we specifically said no ice cream."

Rick added, "Didn't you write that down?"

She pulled out her notepad, looking flustered, searching for their order. "Oh, dear me, I'm so sorry, you're right. I made a mistake. Here, let me take it back for you."

"No, that's quite alright, we've only got so much time and need to get back on the road. Thank you, but no thanks." The impatience in Rick's voice was obvious. Janine simply grinned, and shook her head, wondering at the dolt standing before her. Amber noticed.

"Are y'all sure I can't take them back for you? It's really no trouble at all."

"No dear, we'll just scrape the ice cream off and eat the pie. You can run along and bring us the check in the meantime." Rick watched as Janine embarrassed her, the same way she would do to one of the underachieving students in her class. He liked it. Amber turned away, walking back toward the kitchen. Janine was muttering under her breath about the incompetence of certain people. Rick smirked and shook his head.

They set to eating their pies, the melting ice cream pooling around the edges of the plates. A few of the regular customers had looked over when they were correcting the waitress for her mistake, but they quickly looked away when Rick and Janine returned the stares.

"I have to say," Janine started between mouthfuls, "the pie is really good. It's got a distinct taste to it, even if spoiled with a bit of ice cream. I can't figure out what the ingredients, or what spices are here."

Rick was eating forkfuls of his and finally paused, "Usually, pecan pie is so rich I can only take a few bites of it. This one is rich, but it doesn't seem to be overly filling. Probably the best I've ever had, I'll give them that much." He shoved another forkful in.

Amid the consuming of their pie, they were both startled when an old woman suddenly appeared at the side of their table. They were both so engrossed with eating, that neither had noticed her glide out from the kitchen. She looked ancient, of mixed race, and the lines on her face looked like scars in leather, each crease probably telling its own story from over the years. She wore her salt and pepper hair in cornrows, spilling out the back of a multicolored bandanna. When she spoke, her accent was a strange mixture. They detected Cajun, Native American, Caribbean, and southern drawl.

"I am Granny; they call me Granny Tina. My wandering children," she smiled through yellowed, but straight teeth, "how is your pie?" Rick and Janine had their forkless hands resting on the table. She reached down and gently curled her fingers into their palms. They stiffened at first, but then relaxed. Her hands were rough, worn through the years, yet they felt warm and welcoming. Despite her forwardness, they found themselves smiling at her through mouthfuls of pie. Janine gulped down her bite and said, "It's very delicious, actually."

"Amber—isn't she a wonderful child—said that you had an issue with the way the pie was served?" Her voice was ancient, but clear, and her English impeccable. She continued to smile at them, but not condescendingly, seeming to be genuinely interested in addressing their complaint.

Janine hesitated and found herself stuttering slightly. "Well, it's just that . . . It's just that it came with ice cream after we specifically said no ice cream . . . ." She found her voice trailing off, as if suddenly afraid to assert herself. By this time, they had both finished eating, looking intently at the friendly eyes, the slightly nodding head, and that yellowish smile of reassurance.

"Some of our customers prefer the ice cream on top. It takes some of the edge off the effects of the recipe mixture. However, I can see that you both have very sophisticated palates and would want the full breadth of the dessert. The mixture is secret, handed down through generations, created from scratch. It is legendary. But you can tolerate it."

Rick asked, "The edge off the effects? Legendary? Really . . . ," he hesitated. "Really, there was no problem with the taste at all. It was . . .It was most delicious." He was mesmerized by her smile and demeanor, and her perfect diction. Or was it something else? He suddenly felt slightly dizzy and looked over at Janine. The look she returned told him that she wasn't feeling right either.

She stuttered, looking at the old woman, "I . . . I. . . don't feel quite right. Babe, are you alright?" She looked over at Rick again, and saw that he seemed to be teetering on his chair. "What . . . What is happening?"

Amber and the cooks had come out of the kitchen and were joining Grandma Tina at her side, staring at them. Then customers came down off their counter stools, and others seated at tables came over, offering the slightest of grins and stares, as if they knew what was coming.

Grandma Tina spoke to the two of them. "My children, all will be well, but this trial you must go through. It is for your own good, and for the good of our community."

Rick felt the room spinning now for both of them. They were too weak to get up, their arms and legs numb. Some of the customers, with their wrinkled faces of brown, black, and white, moved to their sides to keep them propped up in the chairs, so they could continue to stare into that ancient face, full of a wisdom that Rick and Janine did not know. Something was about to be revealed.

Grandma Tina's face was a blur, a maelstrom of black and white, yellows and reds, flashes of lightning, and then a vision of pages turning in a history book, shanty towns on fire and a hangman's noose, lines of people waiting at a soup kitchen, small schoolhouses on prairies, and other schools in crowded cities with blackboards that had no chalk for writing, but plenty of cracked, leaking ceilings. They saw people in squalor, squeezing out a living by the sides of swamps, and others, reddish faces, pushed onto reservations with no hope of anything beyond

69

that for home. There were prisoners doing penance for their sins in tiny, stinking cells, and children working in dark, dusty factories.

Then they saw themselves on a hill, staring down in contempt at the poor, the uneducated; the huddled masses, those starving for both food and knowledge.

Through the tempest, they heard snippets of faint, but audible, phrases from Grandma Tina, Amber, and others that were scattered all along Route 301, blending together: *You may not be as smart anymore, but you will be wiser. Don't stop in Staunche for anything. The people up there just ain't right. Some people say Granny's pie is more like a magic spell than a recipe. Stop in and see about our nice, little town here. You can't go through there without leaving something behind . . .*

They came back to consciousness on the shoulder of the road just outside the town limits of Staunche, headed north in the direction of Bailiwick and Interstate 10. Rick was behind the steering wheel of the Acura with Janine by his side. They stared at each other. Rick asked, "Do you like, know what just happened? Like, how we like, you know, got here?"

Janine asked, "Why are you, you know, like, talking like that? Like, what happened back there?"

They sat there for about 15 minutes trying to speak grammatically correct. However, all that came out were "likes" and "you knows" and "aint's" and "youse." Not exactly the speech one would expect to hear from two intense English teachers. Both were on the verge of tears. Janine asked, "What are we, like, gonna do now?"

Rick shook his head. He stared in the rearview mirror, looking back at Staunche, and just said, "I dunno." Turning and staring back at the town, Rick's tears were suddenly stifled. He looked back at Janine and smiled. "But it was, like, such a nice little, like, town, wasn't it?"

She smiled back at him and nodded yes, her own tears now also gone. The stupid grins on their faces seemed to give them an aura that was wonderfully peaceful and content.

Back at Granny's Ham 'N Hash Diner, the wait staff and cooks were in the kitchen gathered around Grandma Tina who sat at a table. A few of the regular customers had joined them. "What should we do with these, Granny?" Amber asked.

Grandma Tina sat in a chair, those around her gently massaging the aching arms and shoulders of her ancient body. She stared down at her apron-covered lap, and at the English textbooks and notebooks that had been confiscated from the car of the two teachers, before they had sent them on their way back north. "Why, child, we can use these in our schools, and out at the prison. These are the most modern learning tools. Children and inmates can be educated from these. The more they learn, the better off they will be in the future, and the better off our little town will be."

Amber smiled; she understood.

Grandma Tina continued, "We just need to find a means to duplicate these to distribute to the inmates. Our town and schools don't have much money to reproduce new books. The world outside of us has high-powered machines that can do so in a short amount of time. Many of the office machines in our buildings are too broken down to do so. But it won't be long. A means to do this will be provided to us in good time."

At that moment the cashier, like Amber, wearing too much lipstick, poked her head in the door. She smiled, "Hey, everybody, Wertz just called and said we have another customer coming in who needs our very best hospitality."

Ten minutes later, Amber fairly skipped over to a small table occupied by a truck driver. He was gruff in appearance, barely acknowledging her as he looked at the menu. From under his baseball cap, he growled, "What's good here?"

Amber offered, "Well the chili's great, and you can never go wrong with the club sandwich."

As he stared at her, she could tell that he was not amused with the colors in her hair, the overuse of lipstick, and the bone jewelry poking out above her eye. He said, "I don't know. Not sure if my stomach can take chili in this heat. Besides, I'm kind of in a hurry."

Amber looked beyond him through the front windows. "Is that your truck out there?"

He glanced again at her briefly and then went back to scanning the menu. "Yes, it is."

"Whatcha' haulin' in it?"

He had a large nose, and his flaring nostrils looked to Amber as if they were sniffing the air. "Not that it's any of your business, little missy, but I've got a load of copying machines. I'm taking them to the University of South Florida, over in Tampa."

Amber took the slightest moment to ponder. "Probably the most modern ones you could get, I bet."

A mocking smile came upon his face. "Yeah, that'd probably be a pretty good bet."

She looked back at him and changed the subject back to his order. "Say, if you're in a hurry, why don't you just have a piece of Granny's pecan pie? Best in the South, you know. Why if you find a better piece of pie, the cook might just come out and step in front of your semi and let you mow him down, he'd be so upset." She snorted at her own joke, again.

The trucker didn't seem amused. "It's lunchtime, I think I need some real food, not pie."

But Amber was so cheery. "Oh, come on now, live a little. Have some dessert before you have the main dish."

He shook his head. "You know, it's funny. That cop back there who pulled me over and then let me go was pushing this pie. You people sure are persistent." For a moment, he considered this smiling young waitress with her too red lips and her tri-colored hair. He lingered a second more. "Oh, what the hell. Bring me the pie with a cup of coffee, black, no cream or sugar.

"Coming right, up, honey," Amber beamed, but he didn't hear her. He had already gone back to ignoring her and taking out his cell phone to make a call. Had he watched her walk away, he might have seen the look in her eye and the smile on her face as she turned in triumph. It was like the smile of a rattlesnake, just as it's about to sink its fangs into you.

Granny Tina would be so pleased with her, with the way she was helping to build up their little town. She had talked another rude person into eating her special pie. She didn't even bother to ask this one if he wanted ice cream with it.

This story is from way back in my childhood. Bodman Park, in Middletown, New Jersey, where this playground was, has long since changed. Not enough open space anymore, too filled with baseball and soccer fields, and snack bars, and loudspeakers announcing ball games, upsetting the quiet of a Sunday afternoon in my old neighborhood just on the other side of the Park, separated by a wooded hill. The playground and the merry-go-round are long gone now, too. But maybe that's a good thing. I would get a chill that I can't quite explain when I was a kid riding on it. It's the same chill that I see in my granddaughter who is hesitant to climb up one of those sliding boards that has a curving tube covering it. It's as if she doesn't want to go down into the brief darkness of that tube, wondering if she's ever going to come out at the bottom. Kids can see things that adults don't. We seem to lose that extra, hidden sense of sight as we grow older. It's one of the things that we need to re-learn from our children.

THE MERRY-GO-ROUND

I went to the park the day they were removing the merry-go-round. Somehow, I thought watching the removal would be a way of getting revenge on what it had done to Alex and me. I didn't care about what it had done to Ricky Makefield.

I watched the men work. The bars, wooden benches and slats came apart easily enough. The stain Alex and I had seen went unnoticed by them. But the center pole embedded in the ground did not come out so easily. They started to pull it out of the ground with a thick chain attached to a backhoe's shovel. At first, there was some resistance, as expected, because it was supposed to be anchored in cement under the clay. But it finally did start coming out. Then more of it came out. "What the hell? How far under does it go?" I heard one of them say. Then I heard them groaning in disgust. There was a stinking ooze coating the pole. Every kind of maggot and grub was clinging to it, as if they were leeching some kind of disgusting existence from it.

After about eight feet of it was exposed, I cried at what came out next. There were long tendrils coming up from the ground, strangling the pole. They looked like elongated fingers and had an evil orange-like glow to them. The public works men shouted and stepped back, nauseated from the stench and malevolence gripping the pole.

The guy operating the backhoe yanked on the controls, and the pole actually snapped. The grubs and maggots and ooze instantly dried up from the section that was snapped off. But the tendrils engulfed the remaining part sticking up from the hellish ground and pulled it back under.

I backed away from the scene on wobbly knees, shaking my head and blubbering. The men were staring in disbelief at the clean piece of pole lying on the ground and the spot where the other piece had been swallowed up. Once more, I ran away from the merry-go-round, wondering how the men would explain what they had seen to the other grownups.

Dr. Edward Phung, my psychiatrist, had been alternatively taking notes and looking up at me as I sat on the couch in his office and recounted to him this childhood terror. He stopped writing, leaned forward in his chair, and gave me a look that could only come from a shrink. He didn't believe me. It was obvious, another grownup who didn't believe.

"Now, Ted, I want you to tell me again about the actual day, that day at the merry-go-round. Tell me again about what happened to Ricky and to Alex, and to you."

I didn't want to go through it again. I suppose this was his way of helping me through the pain, but I didn't think it was working. I leaned back against the couch, exasperated. "Come on, doctor. I've already told you what happened. Why should I go through it again?"

But he shook his head; he was patient and persistent. "Ted, I know this may be hard for you, but I want to make sure I've got my notes straight. I want to find out what really happened to you. This will help."

"What really happened to me? I've told you what really happened. I can't help it if you don't believe it." My voice came out more annoyed than I had intended.

Very gently, "Please, Ted. You've still got a half hour left. If nothing else, it's your money." He smiled, making a joke to get me to lighten up. But I wasn't in a cheery mood. He'd gotten me thinking. He's supposed to be the expert, right? Maybe this *was* something in my mind, and it didn't happen the way I had thought? I should listen to the expert, the grownup. I shook my head, but then I reluctantly told him the account over again.

"I heard some of the kids at school say it's because there was some devil group that performed rituals on it, and that's why it acts so weird, wanting to hurt kids and stuff." My best friend, Alex Williams, was trying to scare me, and it was working, but I was trying not to show it. At twelve, he was two years older than me and a lot more daring. He had this coppery, red hair and freckles, and some of the bigger kids would make fun of him for it. I think that's why he tried to always be so brave, to show he was tough, to show that they couldn't bother him.

"Who . . . who told you that? What kids at school?" I was trying to keep the jitters out of my voice. We were sitting on our bikes by the curbside in front of my house. The bikes were the old stingrays with the banana seats and sissy bars on the back. We used our feet to rock them back and forth on the pavement. It was summer—a warm, humid day. The motion created a small bit of breeze. I looked up. Despite the humidity, the sky was vast and clear. It stretched away forever.

"Oh, you know, just some of the older kids at school. Hey, come on, Teddy, let's go over to the park and check it out."

"Well . . . I don't know, Alex. I don't really feel like it. How about if we take a ride around by the McCarthy's house and go down in the back and check out the creek?"

He stared at me, his expression a mixture of eagerness and bravado. "You're not scared, are you, Teddy?"

I smiled back, "Oh yeah, sure." But his eyes were like drills, delighting in my discomfort. It's funny how even a best friend will enjoy teasing you and watching you squirm. If he can't do it to the older kids, he can do it to his timid buddy.

"You're chicken! Come on, Teddy!" Then he started flapping his arms and making clucking noises.

"Shut up, Alex."

"Bwak, Bwak!"

"Shut up, Alex!" But then I started laughing, maybe because of nerves or maybe because he looked funny flapping his arms wildly and sounding as if he was running around a barnyard.

He laughed, "Alright then, Teddy. Let's go!"

I didn't want to show I was scared. "Yeah okay, Alex, it's no big deal. Let's go on up to the dumb old playground like the little kids do, so we can ride on the stupid merry-go-round."

But my attempt at insulting him didn't work. "Okay, I'll race ya!" With that, he took off up the street toward the park entrance. I pumped the pedals to get after him. The adrenaline was working, and my heart was pounding—but not from the exercise.

A gully had been cut into the wooded hill that separated our homes from the park. The dirt road allowed passage for Township vehicles. This in turn thinned into two dirt paths that the tires had worn through the grass. These led to the playground area. The layout was circular in design. The open, grassy center was exposed to direct sunlight, but the horse swings, monkey bars, slide, merry-go-round and other rides were interspersed among the trees that surrounded the open area. The trees provided good shade on a steamy day.

It was hot enough that day. Apparently, a lot of kids had decided to just stay home and watch the Saturday morning cartoons. That might explain why we were the only ones at the playground. I would have liked to have stayed in and watched cartoons, too, but Alex was at my door early, eager for me to come out and hang with him.

"Don't you want to go on the slide or something else first?" I asked when I pulled up behind him.

"Nope." He jumped off his bike at the merry-go-round, glanced back at me with a grin and then turned to the ride.

It was a simple construction of wood and metal. The wood slats were separated into a six sections by metal bars that ran from the center pole to an outer bar that circled the structure. About six inches below this circular bar and protruding about eight inches out were wooden planks that were connected to the slats. These served as benches that you sat on while holding onto the outer bar with your feet dragging along the ground. Someone had to run along the side, holding onto the bars to get it going. Then they would stop and give the circular bar a push with each revolution, moving it faster, spinning the sky and tree branches above your head.

In those days, long before video games and virtual reality, kids actually went outside and played and hung out together. Our parents didn't watch us so closely. They didn't even really want us home before supper time, so it wasn't unusual that there were no adults at the playground.

Some kids said it was a fun ride. But I didn't like it. I knew of a few kids who had fallen off. Only they claimed they were pulled off, or thrown off, by something unseen. Such stories were just nonsense to the grownups. Our parents knew we would always cover for a friend who had done something reckless that got them hurt. If we weren't going to tell them who really pulled us off the ride, then stop crying about it, Mom would say. Then she would go back to hanging out laundry, and trying to figure out what to make for supper.

The stories from the kids who had been injured, and the older kids that Alex had spoken to, who claimed there was demon worshipping going on at the merry-go-round, only seemed to make him more eager to try it. He climbed up and lay down on the slats in one of the hexagon's triangles. The yellow paint was old, but still had a dull sheen to it. He sat up and looked at me again, smiling at my fear. "You're not going to ride it, are you, Teddy?"

I shook my head no. He just shrugged. "Okay, then, how about giving me a push?" I hesitated, not wanting to touch it.

"Oh come on! Don't be such a baby!"

I didn't want him telling anyone I was a baby. Slowly, I wrapped my fingers around the bar closest to him, expecting to feel something like an electric shock pulse through me. But it just felt cold. I began to slowly walk the ride in motion.

Alex shook his head and laid back down, gazing at the treetops and sky. "Come on, faster, Teddy! Come on!"

It was then that I noticed the stain in the triangle area to his left. It stood out against the paint. I stopped walking and held the merry-go-round still. "What is that?"

Alex sat up, annoyed. I pointed to the stain. In the dappled sunlight it had a reddish, brown hue to it. Alex stared at it for a moment and then looked at me. "You know what that is, don't you, Teddy?" I shook my head no.

"That's where they did it."

"Where who did what?"

He had that stupid grin again. "You know—the devil people. That's where they sacrificed the animals. Only they didn't clean up the blood."

"Oh yeah, sure." I tried to look tough, but he heard the jitters in my voice again.

"No, no, it's true. The older kids at school told me that's what the devil people did." He hesitated a moment, then leered at me. *"They probably even sacrificed some people."*

I didn't say anything. Then he started laughing and threw himself back against the slats. "Oh man, I really had you going! You should've seen your face!"

"Yeah, real funny. You want me to push you faster?" I really wanted to leave the merry-go-round. Just five or so yards either way were the slide and the swings, and the other rides that had no scary reputation. They were a lot more inviting to me.

Alex didn't answer me. "Hey, Alex, do you want to go faster or not? I'm not pushing this thing all day, you know." But he still didn't answer. His eyes seemed to be locked on the sky above.

"Alex? Hey, Alex?"

Still lying on the slats, he glanced over at me—his eyes a combination of wonder and what looked like fear.

"Alex? What's the matter?" He turned and stared back above, holding onto the bars on either side of him.

"It's weird," he said, with a slight shake of his head, "I was just lying here looking up at the sky past the trees, how big it is, how wide it is. It looks . . . bottomless."

"But, Alex, it wouldn't be bottomless. The sky's on the top."

He shook his head again. "But things look different when you're lying here. It's like . . . It's like gravity is different."

"What?"

"It's like you're lying here on the bottom of the world, looking out into space. The sky is space. And you have to hold on, because if you don't, you'll fall off, right through the trees and out into space."

This was too freaky. "Come on, Alex, let's go! This isn't funny." But he wasn't smiling; he wasn't trying to be funny. He sat up and started to move to get off the ride.

"Yeah, okay, Teddy, let's go. . ."

"HEY! Not so fast, kid! I'll push it for ya!"

We both jumped and looked around, startled by the voice. When I saw who it was coming from, I felt as cold as the metal bars in my hands. It was Ricky Makefield. "Pricky Ricky" is what we called him behind his back. He was one of the bigger kids that Alex was talking about, 14 to be exact. He came out from behind a large tree within

83

earshot of us. Despite being the dumb oaf that he was, neither of us had heard him creep up.

He liked to pick on smaller kids. You know the kind. He's the one who'd probably grow up to develop a beer gut from too much booze and crappy food. He'd wind up working some mindless job the rest of his life and marry some trashy, chain-smoking, beer gut wife. He'd exist, instead of live, becoming more and more of a nobody each day until his liver finally gave out, dumping him over like a load of sludge poured into a hole.

That's *probably* what would happen to Pricky Ricky. But right at that moment, he was scary, pure and simple. Right now, there was no beer gut. I remember colors; a rough black tee shirt, soaked in the summer heat, and his grinning, yellowed teeth.

He walked over. "What are you looking at, *Turdy?*" There was no hiding my fear. Like the mongrel that he was, Ricky sensed it. He pushed me over onto the ground, my left elbow hitting hard on the clay. I crawled against a nearby tree. My eyes were watering up as I stared back at Ricky.

He laughed, "Yeah, go ahead and cry, Turdy! Ya little baby!"

Alex was a little braver than me, but I could hear the quiver in his voice, too. "Hey, Ricky, come on. Leave him alone."

Ricky turned away from me and gave Alex a cold stare. Then he flashed those up-to-no-good yellow teeth again. "Tell you what, Alex, looks as though Turdy here is out of it. So, I'm going to be a nice guy and give you a push."

"No, Ricky, I don't think - " He tried to get up, but Ricky pushed him back down to the slats with one beefy arm. He started a slow trot around the merry-go-round, giving it a good push. Alex tried to sit up again, and Ricky pushed him down even harder.

"What's the matter, Alex? Afraid you're going to fall up into the sky?" His laughter seemed to shake the leaves in the branches above. Unable to comprehend how he had heard our conversation, I lay there against the tree, staring in fright as Ricky pushed the merry-go-round faster. Alex's face became a blur, but I saw him as if pleading *help me!* Sorry, Alex, but it seemed a lot safer to just hug that tree and rub my elbow. I did nothing for him.

I wouldn't have thought that any one person could get that ride moving so fast. But the big oaf was surprisingly light on his feet. Alex wasn't looking my way anymore. He was staring skyward, looking as if a train was bearing down on him from out of the blue.

Suddenly, I realized the reason that Alex's eyes looked so scared, and it wasn't because of Pricky Ricky. He was being pulled away from the merry-go-round, *up*, and away from it. Impossibly, he was hovering, defying gravity, just as he had imagined a few minutes before. His hands and their white-knuckle grip were supported by his feet that were hooked around the lower sections of each bar. The rest of his body was straining, trying to lie back down on the slats. But his midsection seemed to be rising away.

"Hey kid, let go of the bars! Let go or I'm gonna make you let go!" Ricky didn't seem to notice the nature-defying significance of Alex's position. He had stopped running and was just occasionally sticking out a hand to push at a bar as the merry-go-round revolved faster. Could he really not see what was happening? Alex couldn't look to me for help anymore. His neck was too strained against the unnatural force pulling at him. I clung to the tree, staring, unable to speak. I didn't want to let go, wasn't sure where my body would wind up if I did.

Then, amazingly, Ricky leapt up onto the spinning ride, his feet landing on the bench adjoining Alex's section. He crouched there holding onto the outer bar as the ride flew by in revolutions. He used one hand to try and dislodge Alex's feet.

"No, Ricky! No, leave me alone!"

"I said, let go of the bars!" He started to reach for Alex's right hand to pry his fingers loose. I could hear Alex crying, begging him to stop. Then something else struck me as I stared at the spectacle. The merry-go-round should be slowing down since Ricky wasn't pushing it anymore, but it wasn't. It actually seemed to be accelerating.

I finally found my voice and screamed, "RICKY! NO ONE IS PUSHING THE RIDE!"

His face a streak as the spinning continued, he turned to look at me. He had been hunched over Alex, holding on to the bar with one hand. With each revolution, I saw that dumb, blurred look on his face, not understanding what I had said.

The continued speed of the merry-go-round and his effort to turn toward me caused him to lose his grip. By the laws of nature, Pricky Ricky should have fallen backwards, the centrifugal force yanking him off onto the ground where he would probably just break his dumbass bone. But there was no law there, neither of nature nor man. There were no police or parents to see the spectacular thing that happened.

Ricky fell up, not away and down. He plummeted through the ever-thinning branches of that pine tree overhanging the merry-go-round. I wasn't sure if the awful snapping sound we heard was just the cracking of branches, or his bones as he crashed upward. Birds scattered, flitting away as his bulk approached from below. Remarkably, he managed to grab onto a thin branch at the top of the tree. Twigs and leaves and dirt and bugs cascaded out around him toward the sky. With both hands, he hung there, his legs stretching up toward the hot sunlight.

This was the first opportunity Ricky had to scream. As he dangled skyward, he finally registered what was happening, looking at his torn and bruised body and at his feet straining toward the clouds. His screams seemed to blow away the debris that fell up into the sky.

Alex still had his own problems holding on for dear life, not wanting to join Ricky. This is when I should have jumped up to finally help him, but I couldn't. I stared at the scene taking place above our heads. I wondered if Alex saw it, too. Across the clear sky there suddenly appeared lightning bolts. Then, just for a moment, there were symbols in the sky: pentagrams, ancient looking swirls, Druid-like. And then there was an inverted cross. I blinked, and they were gone.

Ricky's screaming down to us for help took my eyes away from the signs in the sky. A twig must have trickled up through the branches. Instinctively, he let loose one hand to bat it away from his eyes, his body twisting from the effort. That's when he lost his grip. His remaining hand slipped through the leaves on the branch, and he was suddenly clutching air.

"NO!!! NOOOO!!! MAMAAAA!!!" he screamed as he rocketed skyward. Later, I tried to imagine what it must have been like. Accelerating away from him in a blur, Ricky would see the merry-go-round and other rides. He would briefly see the whole playground and our neighborhood. An expanse of earth stretching away would probably be his final view. His brain would die out as he entered the cloud vapor. In the cold of the atmosphere, I pictured his dead fingers twitching, as if he'd been pulled violently away from his mother.

Back on earth, the merry-go-round began to slow down. Gradually, it ceased spinning. Alex fell back against the wood slats. His fingers were still glued to the metal bars, even as the ride stopped.

He lay there, panting, sweating, and crying in the heat, staring at the twisted and broken branches of the tree above him, and the blue-green sky that had claimed Pricky Ricky. "Alex, you've got to get off now! Alex, do it now!" I whimpered at him.

"No! No! I'm afraid! If I let go, it might start again!" But then a soft wind came, and it seemed to push the merry-go-round very slowly. It couldn't be starting again, could it? Maybe Alex was frightened into believing that, so with a howl he let go, scooting his body under the outer bar and tumbling off onto the clay ground. The ride did not move. The sacrifice had been made; there would be no other required today. Alex gave me one sad, crazed glance and then struggled to his feet. He didn't even go for his bike, but just staggered away, not looking back, whimpering and hugging himself.

I was left alone clinging to the tree, just the merry-go-round and me. Its dull painted slats seemed to glow with satisfaction, but it did not move. Was its appetite satisfied for now? Maybe it would take another victim when it was hungry again? I jumped up on shaky feet, grabbed my bike and sped away home.

I never told my parents what had happened. You know how kids make up such incredible stories, the parents would say. Alex didn't tell his parents either. Then again, he really didn't do any talking at all the few times after that when I saw him. He was always clinging to his mother, and he had such a distant look in his eyes.

His mother knew we had been playing together, and I think she somehow blamed me for his sudden timid behavior. I know his mom and my mom got into a big argument about something over the telephone at one time. Mom said that Alex's parents started having some marital problems because of whatever had happened to Alex. They moved away about a year later, and I never saw him again.

Dr. Phung was taking notes.

"Nobody ever saw Ricky Makefield again either. The police considered him a missing child and made an effort to find him, but it was eventually presumed that he had run away or been picked up by a stranger and had met some terrible fate. Years later, I found out Ricky's father was an alcoholic who used to beat his mother. Maybe that's the reason why they seemed to lose interest after awhile as to what had happened to their son. I guess they had their own problems to deal with. At least Ricky would never grow up and get that beer gut that his old man had."

The doctor shot me an unkind glance. I guess that wasn't a nice thing to say. People would say that, because of the way Ricky's parents were, the way he acted wasn't his fault. He was a product of a bad childhood, that's what the grownups would say. I don't know, maybe. I still hated that kid.

"Eventually, the ride was torn down. There were a few more incidents of kids with broken limbs claiming that they'd been pulled off. There were no lawsuits yet, but the Township didn't want to wait for one to happen. It was determined that the ride was just too dangerous, with or without adult supervision. I already told you what happened the day they tried to pull the thing out of the ground."

Dr. Phung tapped his pen on his notepad and looked at me, contemplating. "Ted, I'm going to suggest something. It might upset you, but I'm asking you to consider it for a moment."

"Go on."

"It's possible that you're substituting this fantastic story about the merry-go-round for something else that really happened."

I shook my head. "I'm not following you. What are you getting at?"

"Well, you have to admit that it is a pretty fantastic story. Let's face it—you're claiming that a supernatural event occurred that day." He gave me a raise of his eyebrows, another shrink move. "It's been my experience that when some people describe an unnatural experience such as this, subconsciously, they are covering up for a traumatic event that actually happened to them."

I frowned and shook my head, not liking where this was going. "What are you suggesting happened instead?"

His soft eyes gave me a long glance. "I believe that something happened there, Ted, but it was committed by human beings. Maybe Ricky did something to Alex and made you watch?"

I kept shaking my head.

"Maybe Ricky did something to both of you, or maybe . . ."

"Maybe what?"

"Or maybe something happened to Ricky. Something that was done by an adult, and you and Alex were forced to watch. You say it was the merry-go-round. It's possible your mind is substituting the merry-go-round for an actual adult that hurt you."

I was angry now. "Look, Dr. Phung, are you trying to say that some kind of sexual assault happened out there that day? Come on, that's ridiculous!"

He lifted his hands in a gesture to calm me down. "But listen to this, Ted. Do you think it's just a coincidence that you started having these nightmares, these memories, over this past year, just after you and your wife have had your first child?"

"What are you talking about?"

"Subconsciously, I think you're afraid that what happened to you could happen to your own child."

I leaned back on the couch, and looked away. At this point he had me about as confused and upset as I could be. He went back to his notes. "Ted, I'm going to refill your prescription so that you can get some sleep. Also, I want to try something different with our next consultation."

"What's that?"

"I want to combine our next two sessions. The park you talked about is not far from where you live now, right?

"About 45 minutes away. Not too far."

"Good, we will combine the sessions and use the time to travel there and visit the scene of the incident. I think it will help us get to the bottom of what's bothering you, of what your subconscious is hiding."

It had happened twenty years ago. There were fewer trees in the park now. Many of them had been replaced by Township administrative buildings. However, although the playground rides were gone, the copse of trees that ringed the open area of the old playground was still there, and there was still a circular bare spot on the ground where the merry-go-round had once spun. Noticeably, no grass was growing where the ride once sat.

I was remotely aware that Dr. Phung had stopped making notes and was asking me a question, although I didn't hear him because I staggered back and stared fearfully at the bare, circular ground.

A strange wind had come up out of nowhere. Maybe it was the filtered sunlight or the shadows from the trees, but the dirt and twigs seemed to form a small twister. It then fattened, getting larger and stretched upward toward the sky. I moved back further, along with Dr. Phung. His soft eyes were bulging. In that storm was the definite shape of a demonic face. The eyes were like that of a wolf, and the v-shaped grinning mouth seemed to mock my fear. Then, instantly, the face changed form. It was the agonized face of a fourteen-year-old kid who used to bully other kids in the neighborhood. I turned again and saw that Dr. Phung's eyes were shut. Then as soon as it had happened, it was gone. There was no wind, no twister, and no faces in the tumult. There were just the silent trees and the clay ground where the merry-go-round had once spun.

"Let's go, Ted." Dr. Phung was already moving quickly toward the car.

"What did you see, doctor? WHAT DID YOU SEE, DOCTOR?" But he would not look back at me. Later, as we drove back to his office, I asked him about it. He claimed that he'd seen nothing and didn't know what I was talking about. But his professional eyes did not look confident anymore. He never offered what he thought my subconscious might be hiding.

I didn't make another appointment to see Dr. Phung after that. What would be the point? But my prescription is running out. I'm not sure I will be able to get any sleep once it does. The nightmares won't stop.

It's easy for grownups to say that it was just an illusion, a trick of the light. But I think a lot about that terrible day and what the merry-go-round did to my friend Alex and me, and to Pricky Ricky Makefield. Most grownups don't want to see or accept such things. But kids know they really do happen

This one is a little bit more on the whimsical side. Our kids actually had some of these mail-order grow-a-frogs. They're not supposed to live more than two or three years, and they're not supposed to be able to breed either. But, just like Frankenstein, things grown in a lab can unexpectedly go awry and take on a life of their own. I'm kind of hoping that the Sci Fi channel will pick this one up and make it into one of their state-of-the-art blockbuster films. Step aside sharks, here come the frogs!

FRANKENFROGS

It had been a year. A year since Irv had released the frogs into the lake, thinking he was finally done with them. But one year was all it took for this disaster to come about, for his town of Feral Brook to become a feeding ground for these two giant, web-footed gluttons.

Was it really just yesterday that the beasts had come up out of the water? The media had descended on their town, like a swarm of flies. *Frogs like to eat flies*, Irv thought to himself.

He hated those frogs. There were so many times that he had just wanted to flush them down the toilet, but how could he bear the look on his daughter's face if he had done so?

Once they switched them from the goldfish bowl to the five-gallon tank, how many different filters had they gone through to try and keep the water clean? At first it was about every three months that he had to clean the tank, but by the time he released them, there were intervals of only a few weeks before the water would be filthy again.

Their amphibious skin that had been shed, food pellets that hadn't been consumed, and all the other pond scum that they generated just from their presence, made it look like an aquatic sty. They seemed to thrive in it. He got the impression that they preferred stinking up his daughter Nancy's room, rather than swimming in pristine water. When catching them in the net and transferring them to the goldfish bowl while he cleaned, he swore that he saw looks of contempt on their Gollum-like faces.

They were such pigs. Irv had come up with various nicknames for them through the years: proggies, priggies, friggies, and fr'hogs. His personal favorite nickname for them, though, was Mr. and Mrs. Amphinity, since it seemed as if they would live forever. In the end, his daughter had gotten the nickname she wanted. Irv had read her the nursery rhyme about Jack Sprat not being able to eat any fat.

"What does that mean, Daddy?" Nancy had asked, so many years ago.

"Well, honey, when it says that his wife could eat no lean, it means that she was very fat."

When they bought the frogs, he was amazed that his daughter had remembered that nursery rhyme from a couple of years before. "Look, Daddy, see how much bigger and fatter the lady frog is? The boy frog is so much skinnier, so we should call them Mr. and Mrs. Sprat."

It was very funny to Irv at that time, that the frogs were a great source of amusement to his daughter. *My, how things had changed*, he thought to himself.

"Oh, no! Irv! Irv, come and see this!" yelled his wife, Eva. Irv ran from sulking at the empty tank in his daughter's room. He stared at the television screen. *They are so hungry.* They had always been, especially the big female, always hungrier than the male. "Now look at what she's eating," Eva said.

On the flat screen was news footage of the female. He could tell it was her because of the coloring—lighter green than the male. The network preceded the clip with the warning that what you were about to see was very graphic. In slow motion was a replay of the female rampaging through town. A cop was firing his gun at her from behind his parked cruiser. Her tongue lashed out and gobbled him down, as if he was some cartoon-like fly in a black uniform. There was no sound as they replayed the scene, but even if there were, no one would have heard him scream because it probably happened so fast. They blurred the screen just before he went down her throat, gun, uniform, and all. He knew it was wrong, but Irv couldn't keep from giggling at the sight. "Uh oh! No more donuts for him."

Eva stared at her husband. "You think that's funny, Irv?" No, it wasn't very funny. However, with the madness that was going on in town, how else to deal with it? Don't people start laughing at the most inappropriate times to deal with madness?

There was a knock at the front door. Irv and Eva looked at each other. The news programs had said that the police had declared a state of emergency, and people were told to stay indoors. Irv opened the door and saw a uniformed police officer standing there, with two other official-looking individuals with him. He was not surprised to see them; he knew why they were there. He just didn't think it would be so quickly.

"Sir, are you Irving Tremont?" the cop was reading from a notebook in his hand.

"Yes, yes, I am."

The officer looked up from his notes. "Can we ask you some questions, Mr. Tremont?"

"What's this all about, officer?"

A stocky woman in a gray pants suit stepped forward. "I'll take it from here, Officer Gomez." Officer Gomez took a step back. "Mr. Tremont, I'm Detective Shoemaker," she croaked, as she pulled out her shield. She had a tough voice, but Irv thought she was mildly attractive, in a well-fed farmer's daughter sort of way.

Eva came forward, "Irv, what's wrong?"

"You folks obviously know what's going on out there. Do you mind if we come in and talk?" Detective Shoemaker asked.

Eva looked at the detective, not liking the way she seemed to be eyeing Irv up and down. "Well, I don't know. What's this all about?"

"Eva, it's okay. It's over. We know why they're here. Please come in, and I'll try and answer your questions." Irv nodded for them to come in.

"Irv, I don't know. We shouldn't just . . ."

"Ma'am, your husband just said it was okay for us to come in. Please don't make this difficult." Detective Shoemaker's voice was bossy. Eva fumed as the strangers walked past her. At least Officer Gomez tipped his hat. "Nice place you have here," he mumbled.

Eva spewed at them, "Does anyone want any coffee?" She glared at her husband. They all shook their heads "no."

Detective Shoemaker introduced the third person. "Mr. and Mrs. Tremont, this is Dr. Bushkill. He is a biology professor from the University over at Rochester. He's here to help us try and kill these frogs." It was an introduction hinting of disdain. It occurred to Irv that Detective Shoemaker would probably just like to go at the frogs with machine guns and rocket launchers, and forget about how the good professor would like to go about disposing of them.

Dr. Bushkill addressed Irv, "Mr. Tremont, it's become obvious that these were no ordinary frogs, none that we know of that would grow to such a size through simply natural means. We, uh, I mean the police, were able to do some research into companies that grow live animals in laboratories. They found the River Tree Company in Florida, and by making a simple phone call were able to determine that you have been the only person in this part of upstate New York for years who has ever purchased their frogs. You have kept in contact with them by periodically buying food for the frogs through the years. Is that correct?"

Irv thought of Dr. Bushkill as the type of man who, when not tromping around in a marsh, enjoyed all the trappings of being a college professor, especially when it came to wearing a tweed jacket with a turtleneck underneath. He probably smoked a pipe too. "Yes, it's true."

Detective Shoemaker asked, "You must know, Mr. Tremont, that these frogs are not ordinary animals. They had to have been genetically engineered to grow to such an enormous size. Do you know anything about how these frogs got into the lake?"

Irv shifted his eyes back and forth between Officer Gomez, Detective Shoemaker and Dr. Bushkill. Shoemaker again, "Mr. Tremont, did you release the frogs into the lake?"

"Irv, you don't have to tell them anything," Eva interrupted. "We should probably talk to a lawyer first."

Detective Shoemaker blurted, "Mrs. Tremont, please!"

Eva wheeled on her, "Oh shut up, you fat troll!" Officer Gomez let out a little chuckle, and then stifled himself when Shoemaker glared at him.

Irv cut in, "Eva, Eva, please, it's alright. It's pretty obvious they know the truth. We don't want to make things worse than I already have."

Eva was still staring down Detective Shoemaker. The detective, in turn, looked like she wanted to take a hammer and do something to Eva's face with it. But she let it go when Eva shook her head and walked a few steps away.

Calmly, Dr. Bushkill asked, "Mr. Tremont, can you tell us what happened? Can you answer some questions about the frogs? It might help us to figure out how to stop them." Irv nodded and then directed them to follow him into their daughter's room.

In Nancy's room, Irv showed them the empty five gallon tank. Detective Shoemaker, Officer Gomez, and Dr. Bushkill looked around the girl's bedroom. It was typical of a teenage girl, pictures of friends and hunky-looking actors on the walls, a dresser strewn with makeup and cheap jewelry. Officer Gomez picked up a necklace with Native American designs on it.

Eva came into the room and asked bluntly, "Would you mind putting that down?" It's a very precious piece to my daughter. There's a matching bracelet she sometimes wears with it."

"Nice," Gomez said. He set the necklace down on the dresser. "Mrs. Tremont, where is your daughter? We had told everyone to stay indoors until we can safely deal with the frogs."

Eva nodded. "She's at a friend's house over on Willoughby Drive, by the lake. She slept over there last night. When we heard the sirens going off and turned on the horrible news and found out what was happening, we called her and told her to stay indoors over there until everything was safe again. She was crying and wanted to know if they were her frogs. But I told her to stay indoors at Rachel's house and we would come and get her when the crisis was over."

For a moment, Eva seemed to be thinking about something. "She loved those frogs. She said they would sit and watch her through the tank as she sat at her dresser putting on makeup."

Gomez nodded at her. "Did you say she was staying over on Willoughby Drive?" he asked, and then seemed to pause for a moment, thinking about something.

"Officer Gomez? Would you come here please? I need you to take some notes." It was Detective Shoemaker. She and the professor were standing by the empty frog tank asking Irv questions. Gomez walked over, as Eva listened in on them.

Shoemaker said, "So, tell us what happened, Mr. Tremont."

Irv sighed and started. "We bought the frogs through the company in Florida . . . ."

"River Tree?" Dr. Bushkill asked.

"Yes, River Tree, of course." *You already knew that, idiot.* For a college professor, the guy seemed like a real dolt to Irv.

"Anyway, we bought the frogs after seeing them advertised in a magazine. They ship them live as little frogs already, not even tadpoles. Nancy was two at the time. We thought they would make an unusual Christmas present. Little did we know that they would live for so many years—we figured two or three years at most before they would croak."

Officer Gomez giggled a little again at the unintended pun. Shoemaker shot him a glare.

Irv continued, "Well, anyway, I kept on periodically ordering the food. They got to know me well enough when I would call down there for a new order: 'Same credit card, Mr. Tremont? You want the deluxe package with the extra bottle of food for free, the usual, sir?' That kind of thing.

"Well, I always had to take care of them. My daughter couldn't lift the tank to take it outside and dump it, not with five gallons of water in it. They would dirty it up and stink up her room. Quite frankly, they got to be a real pain in the ass. I kept hoping they would just die, but I think those things could withstand a nuclear blast."

Dr. Bushkill asked, "Was there anything unusual you could tell us about them, Mr. Tremont?"

Irv thought for a moment. "Well, they're not supposed to be able to breed, or so the company claimed."

"They are asexual?"

"If that means that they don't have sex, then yes, they are supposed to be asexual."

"And?" Bushkill pressed him.

"And they mated and bred. I went on the website for the company. It was littered with accounts from other customers who had said their lab frogs had babies. We noticed them one day, like tiny tadpoles. We figured they would grow up also, so maybe we'd have to get a 10 gallon tank. But it seemed like the next day they were gone. We didn't notice any little bodies floating around dead. It was obvious that the two frogs ate them. I expect the female ate the majority of them. She's real hungry, obviously no mothering instincts whatsoever."

102

At this, Bushkill seemed to change his expression, slowly nodding and stroking his chin, like some kind of bobble-headed Einstein, only without the frothy moustache. "Anything else unusual?"

Irv shook his head no.

"So, what finally happened, Mr. Tremont?" Detective Shoemaker asked.

Irv hesitated. He looked over at Eva. The others looked at Eva, too. She had her head down. She had let him do it. She didn't want him to, but she hadn't stopped him either. They never told their daughter the truth.

Shoemaker looked back at him. "Come on, Mr. Tremont, continue, please."

Irv was ashamed. "I . . . Nancy went away for a week about a year ago, on vacation with the family of one of her girlfriends. I got fed up with taking care of the little bastards. It was a bad week of work, and I was busy with other stuff around the house for the weekend. I didn't feel like taking the time to clean the tank again. I wanted to just flush them down the toilet, but I felt I owed it to my daughter to at least give them a fighting chance. We just told her they had finally died while she was away."

Shoemaker said, "So instead, you took them out to Speckled Lake and you dropped them in. Is that right?"

"Yes, that's right. I figured they would either frolic and eat flies to their hearts content in their swamp water, or be a quick snack for a bass or snapping turtle. Either way I didn't care."

"You didn't care?" Shoemaker accused him. "You didn't care? You've never heard what can happen to the environment when you introduce a species that's not indigenous to the area?" She looked at him as if he was someone she could push around and would love doing so. She said, "I'm sure Dr. Bushkill can confirm what I just said about non-indigenous species."

Irv was annoyed. He supposed that Detective Shoemaker had probably never even heard the word "indigenous" before she met Dr. Bushkill. He said, "How was I supposed to know this would happen—that this could happen? They're just two dumb frogs."

Dr. Bushkill interjected. "Mr. Tremont, these animals were cloned in a lab. However, that doesn't mean that they wouldn't be able to take on elements of those created in nature. You saw for yourself the way they were able to breed without supposing to be able to do so. Nature has a way of breaking through these barriers.

"In addition, you saw how once you introduced them to a larger living space, they got larger themselves. The combination of them using the elements of nature, and the genetics that the lab gave them, has allowed these creatures, in an even larger environment, to increase their size and mass proportionately to that environment. Essentially, they were created as little monsters in a lab and have now grown to be monsters the size of a school bus out in the wild."

Irv turned away from all their looks. He didn't want to answer any more of their questions. He muttered, "How was I supposed to know all this would happen? And why did they come up out of the water, anyway? Why couldn't they just stay in there?"

Bushkill said, "They probably consumed most of the larger species that are in the lake. There are plenty of locals who fish all the lakes around these counties, and there have been many reports of low catches, especially here at Speckled Lake. There would be some larger and smaller fish left, but it would be increasingly difficult for the frogs to catch them because of dwindling numbers. Simply put, they occupied the deepest parts of the lake, surfacing only briefly for air. This would explain why no one had ever seen them before. They came up out of the lake because there was a fresh food source. It's a whole lot easier for them to catch overweight, lumbering humans than tiny, fast fish." Bushkill glanced briefly at Detective Shoemaker.

"What are you looking at me for?" she asked.

Eva came over to Irv at that moment and put her arms around his waist. She turned to face the others. "I don't think we're going to answer any more questions from you people until we have a lawyer with us."

Detective Shoemaker shrugged and glanced at Officer Gomez. Dr. Bushkill sighed, "Just one more thing, Mr. Tremont, please. Can you tell me what this is?"

Irv looked from Eva to Bushkill, who was holding a plastic cylinder with small crystals in it. "They are crystals that you're supposed to add to every gallon of water used. They're supposed to take the fluoride out of the water. I guess the fluoride is not good for the frogs' constitution."

Bushkill nodded and stroked his geeky chin again, deep in thought.

Officer Gomez had wandered back over to Nancy's dresser in the awkward moment when Eva had said they wanted a lawyer. He picked up a wrinkled piece of loose leaf that had writing on it. "Can I ask you something, Mr. Tremont?" Irv was exasperated, "What is it, Officer?"

105

Gomez was grinning. "Can you tell me what this is?"

Irv walked over and grabbed it out of the cop's hands. Reading it, he started grinning himself. It was something funny he could dwell on, despite all the misery he had caused. "It's a little poem I wrote for Nancy when we first got the frogs, so that she could sing to them when she fed them every morning."

He handed it back to Gomez, who read it again and chuckled at the words:

> Oh, you fat, fat, froggy woggy guys,
> with your bulbous, bulging, froggy woggy eyes,
> Here's a wonderful breakfast surprise, some delicious, dehydrated flies,
> Oh, you lucky fat, fat, froggy woggy guys.

Then Gomez stopped chuckling, paused, and looked up at them. "Mrs. Tremont, where did you say the house is where your daughter is staying?"

"Over on Willoughby Drive, I told you."

Gomez looked quickly to Shoemaker and Bushkill. They both suddenly seemed even more concerned.

Irv and Eva noticed it. "What is wrong, Officer?" Irv demanded.

Shoemaker cut in. "Mr. Tremont, I think you and your wife better come with us. You see, on the way over here, on the police radio, the report was that the male was making its way along the grassy way that lines Willoughby

106

Drive. There's a creek that runs adjacent to the street there, so we believe that's why it was in that area. The news reports were that people were coming out of their houses, trying to get a picture of it before it got too close to them. The police and fire departments have been trying to get the people to stay in their homes."

Eva started whimpering at first, and then was crying as Irv half carried, half pushed her to the waiting squad car outside.

Officer Gomez gunned the black and white through the residential streets, with his lights on and siren wailing. They made Willoughby Drive in about three minutes. All jumped out of the car as they parked it in front of a church. There was a crowd gathered across the street. They could all see why.

"Don't these people have the sense to stay away from here?" Officer Gomez shouted. "Being swallowed by a giant frog is a pretty terrible way to die. You people get back away from there!" he yelled, as he emerged from the squad car. The throng seemed mesmerized by the giant amphibian as it lumbered up the greenbelt of grass that lined the residential street. The crowd had gathered when they had heard it was on this side of town—cell phone cameras snapping away to capture an image of the phenomenon.

"Where's Nancy, where's my Nancy!" Eva screamed. Out of the car, she started to run over toward the crowd, but Irv yanked her back.

"We'll find her, Eva, calm down! We'll find her!"

The male continued plodding along the grass next to the creek. Collectively, the crowd must have thought that he seemed a safe way off yet, but in the next moment he hopped into the air. It was an incredible sight to Irv. The frog seemed suspended in midair for a moment, its white belly blocking out the sky, like some huge, deflating, hot air balloon coming down. Irv barely heard the screams from the stupid onlookers across the street, as it came down, crushing a dozen of them under its gelatinous body. Several other people were propelled up and then down onto the grassy area from the force of the frog's landing. They scrambled to get up and run. The frog's tongue flickered out and snagged a young woman. She wriggled like some tortured meal worm as the frog sucked her back into its mouth.

A beer-bellied guy, too slug-like to make any real speed, was next. "No! No! I don't want to die!" The tongue wrapped around his legs. He managed to get his hands around the pole of a speed limit sign as he was dragged along the ground. He held on just for a moment. "No, no!" The frog suddenly snapped its head to the right, yanking him away from the pole. The sound was like a bullwhip cracking, as bones shattered inside his body. An instant later, his screams were swallowed up as he went down the frog's throat.

Suddenly, the big male turned its body toward their direction. The eyes were glassy, liquid orbs, measuring the distance that its tongue could reach. Officer Gomez, Detective Shoemaker, Dr. Bushkill, Irv and Eva all saw it. "No!" Eva cried out, forgetting about her Nancy for the moment. "He's coming for us!" Gomez let out a barrage of swearing, and they all started running—except for Irv. They made for the entrance of the small church.

The frog didn't move right away. Irv thought, *did it just cock its head toward me?* The bulbous eyes glared directly at him, as if in recognition. Weren't they just stupid frogs, born in a lab? All those years they must have resented him, every time he disturbed them from their filthy swamp of a tank to change the water. Knowing that he hated them, were they sizing him up, building their wrath, *remembering* him, if this day should come?

Just before the frog leapt, Detective Shoemaker dug her hands into Irv's shoulders and yanked him back to get him running. "Let's go, Mr. Tremont. Time is short." As they turned and began running behind the others, Irv suddenly heard Eva screaming about the male jumping. He felt a large shadow overtake them. They all let out a freakish howl as they instinctively hit the ground anticipating the slimed body crushing them to death.

But the crush didn't come. The shadow passed over, and they heard a loud splat, like a side of beef being sawed in half. Suddenly it rained heavily just for an instant. But it wasn't rain water. Irv heard his wife screaming again. He looked up and saw her stand, her whole body shaking. She was covered with huge spots of blood—the frog's blood. They all were. He looked down at his own arms and hands. They were speckled with the berserk lab animal's blood, and, here and there, with tidbits of its flesh.

Now Eva was screaming again, looking up at the top of the church. Officer Gomez and Detective Shoemaker were yelling at her to shut up. They were trying to get the shreds of the frog off their clothes. The male belched out one final croak that vibrated in Irv's ears. Its body had been ripped nearly in two, the steeple of the church sticking up through its midsection, dripping amphibious viscera.

Amid the gore, Irv started laughing. "He's dead! He's finally dead!" Eva came sobbing over to him, wrapping her slimed body around his waist, falling to her knees.

"Un-freaking believable," Detective Shoemaker muttered. "He must have leapt with too much force. He overshot us and landed right on top of the church. Can you believe that?" she asked Dr. Bushkill. "It was just kind of crawling along, and then it leapt on top of those people. How can it do that?"

Dr. Bushhkill was shaking visibly. Maybe it was from the cold frog plasma that coated him, but probably not. He'd gone on field trips to study animals of various regions during his years in academia, but was never prepared for this. "I don't know. He's a frog, after all, Detective. They can jump, you know. Maybe because of their huge mass they know that too much jumping would cause a strain and they would collapse their mass upon themselves, so they do it sparingly. I don't know . . . ."He sat down in the wet grass, pulling shreds of the beast's flesh away from his snappy, tweed jacket.

Officer Gomez just shook his head in disbelief. Behind him, the remaining crowd of onlookers, who were just lucky enough not to get killed, was gathering. There were shouts of "eewwws!" and "yuck!" and "that's so gross!" and "who's going to clean that up?" They all seemed to have lost any concern for the twelve crushed bodies across the street. The smelly body of the big male covering the roof of the church was a lot more fascinating.

Irv was helping Eva to her feet. He said, mostly to himself, "His rage got the better of him. His anger gave him too much force." Officer Gomez heard him and nodded.

110

Eva was crying, "Irv, where is Nancy? We've got to find Nancy! I need to see her Irv, please!"

"Alright, alright, Eva, we will. Let's start over to Rachel's house. I'm sure she's there . . . ."

He stopped in the middle of his sentence, and looked up at a loud, belching noise coming from the dead frog. It's very exposed belly was spewing forth partially digested contents—including the victims it had just consumed. Pieces of bodies were spilling off the roof of the church onto the grass below, including the mangled remains of the beer belly guy and the willowy young lady. The crowd behind was now screaming in horror—some retching up their lunches.

And then, one more thing fell out. It was a forearm. The frog's digestive processes had severed the arm at the elbow away from the rest of the body. It was a young woman's forearm, a teenage forearm, with a bracelet around the wrist. The bracelet had a completely recognizable, unmistakable, Native American design to it.

Above all the other noise Irv heard were his wife's screams avalanching through his ears. It was the last sense he remembered as the world started spinning and he and Eva crumpled to the ground.

In the downtown area, the larger female was still hungry. The police officer that she had consumed live on camera earlier was just one of many snacks. Amazingly, as she rampaged down Main Street, people were still sticking their heads out of windows, peeking out from alleys, speeding away in news vans, all the while snapping pictures of her to viral them out for the world to see what was happening in Feral Brook. It was chaotic. It might as well have been the Running of the Bullfrogs. Police on bullhorns were shouting at the citizens to get indoors— unwilling to fire at the female because of the chance of hitting an idiot bystander.

But why would the police expect the scene to be any different? After all, they know that no one in this curious crowd would expect that they would be the one to get eaten by the giant amphibian; things like that always happen to someone else. That's why the cops shouldn't have been surprised by the bald-headed 19-year old who suddenly raced out on his skateboard from a side street and crossed the female's path. He and his pimply buddies had just finished off a bottle of vodka swiped from a home liquor cabinet and chased it with a couple of cans each of an energy drink named "Zombie Javalanche." There was so much caffeine in just one can of the product that a tortoise drinking it would probably do back flips.

After they'd finished drinking, they headed downtown to see the spectacle. The cops seemed helpless, but this skateboard dude, Vinnie, with his demonic tattoos on his arms and the fake diamond stud poking out from just under his lower lip, knew he could do it. It occurred to these soused, young lads that the empty liquor bottle would serve perfectly as a Molotov cocktail with which to kill the beast. They would slay the dragon and be heroes, and probably earn some reward money. That would buy a lot of alcoholic and caffeine drinks, and probably get them in good standing with some of the babes in town, too.

The others had taunted Vinnie into doing it, and he had finally accepted the challenge. The cops were yelling at him on bullhorns to get away, but Vinnie couldn't hear them—his high, and his own primal scream, drowning out all other sounds around him.

Remarkably, he maintained his balance on the skateboard. As he leaned back slightly to hurl the Molotov, the big female's tongue lashed out and wrapped around his dirty jeans. As he was sucked up toward her mouth, he let out a scream, "NO DUDES, IT'S NOT SUPPOSED TO BE THIS WAY!" Just before he rode that final curl into her mouth, looking upside down, he saw his drunken and high friends in the alleyway. Some of them had dropped jaws at what they were seeing. The others were laughing at him.

The skateboard shot away, and the Molotov slipped out of his hands. As he disappeared in her maw like the fruit fly that he was, the bottle landed on the street, floating just under a police van that the cops had brought downtown. It was parked there to pick up those who wouldn't get off the street, and then had been abandoned at the spot as the big female proved too big to bring down with just their Glocks and shotguns. There was a terrific whoosh as the vehicle exploded, flew into the air, and crashed down on its side in the middle of the street.

A reporter in the opposite alleyway, who had gotten too close because he wanted to get a great picture, was engulfed in the flames. He looked like some scorched marshmallow on legs blistering in the fire as he fell to the ground. The noise of his searing flesh was loud enough to drown out his screams.

Yet Vinnie, riding his skateboard like a suburban surfer, he of the evil tattoos and facial costume jewelry, had accomplished his mission, giving his life for the town in the process. The flames did manage to reach the big female. She let out a giant croak that sounded like a smoldering

113

fart, as the fire arched through her left rear leg. She tried to hop away from the inferno, but couldn't, as she was essentially barbecued to the bone on her left side. Instead, she crashed to her left, right into a bistro that specialized in small, daintily laid out artsy food at outrageous prices.

Watching the now fully burning, violently shaking female destroy the bistro in flames, was Officer Gomez, who had raced over from Willoughby Drive to help out at this scene of carnage, leaving Detective Shoemaker and the good professor to deal with the blubbering, now insanely hysterical Tremonts. Seeing that the giant, burning amphibian had destroyed the bistro, he grinned and said to himself, "Good riddance, I hated that place with its brie and berry plates anyway. It didn't even have a normal grilled cheese sandwich on the menu."

Later that evening, Detective Shoemaker and Professor Bushkill were leaving the hospital together. "Are we just going to leave them there?" Bushkill asked.

Shoemaker stopped on the sidewalk outside the main entrance of the hospital. "There's really nothing else we can do. The medical professionals will have to take care of them now, get in touch with other family members. You saw them yourself. She was basically catatonic, and he just kept muttering that stupid nursery rhyme to himself, 'Oh you big fat froggy woggy guys, with your bulging, froggy woggy eyes,' that sort of thing."

She was grinning about it. Bushkill didn't seem as amused. He shook his head and said to her, "I guess that's what happens when your only daughter wanders out to see about the well-being of her giant mutated pets and then gets indifferently swallowed up by one of them."

114

Detective Shoemaker was getting into her car to head back to police headquarters. The reports for this mess were going to take her into the next morning to complete. She watched Dr. Bushkill getting into his car. "Hey, Professor?" she asked. Bushkill leaned out from his driver's side window. "With the female dead now, we should be done with this, right?" Shoemaker's voice had kind of a pleading quality to it.

Bushkill got back out of the car and seemed to stare past her for a moment. He had that pondering, academic look to his face again. "Well, there are a couple of things bothering me, detective."

"Oh, and what are those?"

"You remember those crystal pellets that were in the daughter's room?"

"Yeah, what about them?"

"Well, Mr. Tremont said they were used to take the fluoride out of the water, remember?"

Shoemaker nodded, "Yes, I remember."

"That lake out there, Speckled Lake, where the two giant frogs emerged from, also serves as a reservoir for the town here. The water is sent through a filtration plant, of course, before it reaches the households. Since it is a reservoir, as was common practice decades ago, the local authorities introduced fluoride into the water to fight tooth decay."

"What's that got to do with anything?" Shoemaker asked.

"Detective, although the fire killed the big female, I think she was already dying."

"How so?"

Bushkill continued, "Did you notice that the big female wasn't hopping anymore? She was pretty much just lumbering around at the end, before she was cooked, as if she didn't have the energy to hop at all. The two mutant frogs couldn't handle the sudden infusion of fluoride into their system. Remember when I said about the male not jumping so often that maybe he didn't trust his mass?"

Shoemaker nodded again.

Bushkill continued, "I think both of the frogs were being gradually worn down by the infusion of fluoride into their systems. The local authorities knew that the rapid addition of fluoride would kill all the species in the lake, so it was introduced gradually, enabling the indigenous aquatic life the time they needed to build up a resistance to it in case they would have a negative reaction.

"For these frogs, on the other hand, the fluoride was a sudden shock to their system. The reports from downtown were that the female seemed to be slowing down even before she got charbroiled. She wasn't hopping anymore. I think the fluoride would have killed them both eventually."

Shoemaker seemed incredulous. "Fluoride? Are you kidding me, Doc? You really think fluoride that comes in toothpaste would do that to those creatures?"

Bushkill nodded yes. "It's not so farfetched. There were studies done in the past when fluoride was first being introduced into drinking water as to whether there would be harmful effects to any aquatic organisms. One such study showed a detrimental effect to the growth of certain species of frogs. Again, the authorities believed a gradual introduction of the fluoride would offset any possible harmful effects. With these mutant frogs, even though they were growing by consuming so much aquatic life in the lake, they were also taking in so much of that fluoride."

Detective Shoemaker thought for a moment and then shrugged, "So what's the problem? What's bothering you?"

Bushkill shook his head. "The thing that is bothering me is that these two adults may have produced offspring again."

"But Tremont said they couldn't reproduce."

"No Detective, he said they weren't supposed to, but they managed to find a way to do it anyway."

Shoemaker was now stroking her own chin. "Yeah, but if that's true, then any offspring would eventually die from the fluoride also, right?"

Bushkill's face was grim. "Just like the other aquatic life, I believe the next generation of these frogs, if there is one, will have adapted to the fluoride in the water and won't be affected by it. They will have built up a resistance."

He seemed to ponder a moment, and then shook his head, "Well, I'm really reaching with that theory." He chuckled to himself, "She probably would've eaten any offspring, anyway. As Mr. Tremont said, 'she had no motherly instincts.'"

Shoemaker forced a laugh, "Yeah, you got that right." She looked in the direction of Speckled Lake. *What are the chances?* However, she was too hungry to think about it now. The last 48 hours had built up an appetite. The police reports could wait; her stomach was what mattered at the moment.

She looked at Bushkill. He looked pretty good to her right now in his tweed jacket, even with the mutant dead frog stains on it. "Hey, Doc, I'm going somewhere to get something to eat. You want to go? I'm thinking that I've got a craving for seafood."

Bushkill shook his head no as he climbed back into his car. "I think I'll pass this time, detective. Thank you. Just don't make it frog's legs, okay?"

She was disappointed that he had turned down her invitation, but let out a hearty laugh anyway. "Good one, Doc."

Bushkill pulled out of the hospital parking lot to head back up to Rochester and his own reports. Then Detective Shoemaker stopped laughing and again looked grimly out in the direction of Speckled Lake.

Out in the deepest part of the lake, a white, globular mass stuck to vegetation at the bottom, about 100 feet from the surface. A large pike, at about five feet, unusual in size even for a lake in upstate New York, moved in for what seemed to be some easy-picking eggs to feed on. Just before it struck the embryonic mass, the eggs burst open, and a good litter of about fifty frogs, in the last stages of being tadpoles, each already a foot and a half long, sped away in the murk.

The pike was disoriented for a moment at the flash of activity rushing past it, just enough time for all the offspring to escape its snapping jaws. Then it seemed to simply shrug off the lost meal as it began to move away. It sensed that the two large predators were gone. Now, as the apex predator in the lake once again, it would be just a matter of time before it would secure a meal.

Suddenly, its body was being pulled in different directions. Its gnashing teeth caught only water as sandpaper-like tongues wrapped around it. The frog/tadpoles were already losing their tails, as each one ripped a piece of the hapless pike into their slimy, juvenile mouths. Like sprinkles of salt in the water, the pike's scales dimly reflected the light from the surface—the only remnants left of the nasty fish. They were scattered in the murk as the frogs propelled away.

The offspring of Mr. and Mrs. Sprat were growing quickly in both size and hunger. They would eat either fat or lean, it didn't matter to them.

I love dark bars that have a huge selection of craft beers, especially dark craft beers. The beers themselves seem to cast shadows around the dusky atmosphere, so that no one can really see your business, or where your eyes might be roving. The idea for this story came from being in one such place. I'll give you a hint about where it is located. If you look for a tavern that just might be in Croydon, Pennsylvania, and that just might be in front of a train station, and that just might include as part of its name an animal from the canine family and an animal from the bovine family, you just might be close. But I don't want to give too much away. You'll find it for yourself. The owner/bartender of the place very much resembles the proprietor in this story, except that the real-life guy is a lot more congenial. Yes, there have been stories about spooky trains, and stories about spooky taverns. Aha, but has there ever been a story about a spooky tavern in front of a spooky train station? Hmm. Yeah, probably. But this is my take on that theme.

LAST STOP TAVERN AND GRILLE

He had passed this place on several occasions on his way home—those couple of times when he had spent a few hours in a cheap motel with a willing co-worker who was tired of her husband. Another time was just after he had been with a lonely lady from one of the bars along the way when, after a few drinks, he had done her right in the parking lot in the back seat of his car. Or was it her car? He couldn't remember; no matter. Max Bailer was a pretty good-looking guy, but when it came to class, he was hideous. Whatever it took to get a woman to give it up was fine with him, whether in a motel, a parking lot, or in a stairwell, he didn't care.

The ones he'd had from the office had told their husbands that they were working late that night. Max always used the same excuse with his own wife. She knew he had a busy marketing job, but whether she believed the working late excuse didn't matter, she always let it go. The two kids at home seemed to keep her content. Mom was their rock. It wouldn't bother Max if his two pre-teen daughters simply thought of their dad as someone who went to work in the morning and, if he got home in time to do so, would eat dinner and then give them a perfunctory kiss on the forehead at bedtime. For Max, and probably for his wife, marriage seemed to have become something of a convenience, rather than a commitment. She drew strength only from her children, as there was no other source.

As he closed the car door and headed for the bar entrance, he wondered why he had never stopped in this place before. *Last Stop Tavern and Grille* was what the dull neon sign said. Maybe because those other times it was late in the evening when he passed by, and he was just tired, trying to stay awake, driving home from a motel with a few drinks in him, and his fluids spent on the woman he had left behind. Or, maybe it was the seedy look of the place because of the old train tracks directly behind the building.

Whatever the reason, he was going to give this place a try tonight. He needed a drink and something to eat, and he was horny—again. Besides that, it was always good to make his moves in varied places, so that he didn't become a regular anywhere. You never know when some nosy neighbor might recognize you and report your activities to the old lady at home.

He opened the door and felt the warmth as he stepped inside, shaking off the early autumn, slightly chilly evening. On either side of the door stood two large, bald bouncers, wearing black short sleeve shirts to show off their biceps, and casual, black jeans. They both seemed to smile in unison at him, through their very white teeth. Their contrasting ebony skin made the teeth look luminescent. The one on his right said, "Good evening, sir. Have a wonderful time tonight." Max just nodded, looking at the size of those biceps, and thinking that he'd better have a wonderful time, or the guy might just hold it against him.

He surveyed the scene, taking in the personality of the place and the vibrations of the crowd. A mirror behind the bar reflected the usual bottles of liquid sin. The lone bartender wore a black tee shirt with something written on it that Max couldn't read from this distance. The guy had thick, curly dark hair, a bushy beard and mustache, and hairy arms to match. Except for his pale face, he looked like a pudgy, black bear.

The place was busy, which Max had expected, due to the number of cars he had seen in the parking lot. There were several waitresses milling about, also dressed in black tee shirts that had the bar's name written on them, and dark jeans, which matched their black hair. Funny, they all wore that same color; it must be some kind of uniform.

The place smelled of good burgers, with the aroma of the juices oozing from fatty, griddled beef. That was stuff that he knew he shouldn't eat, but the scent that slithered through his nostrils was making it too tempting to resist.

The lights were dim; that was good. There was some strange, exotic, Asian crap playing over the sound system, but he didn't care about that, and he didn't care about burgers not being healthy for him. The hunger was strong tonight, and he yearned for a burger and more.

Let's see. Where is she? To his right, the first one to catch his eye was another one wearing a black tee shirt. She was sitting alone at a small table close to the door. Maybe she was the type who would be drinking hard cider, Max thought. She looked rather Goth with her tar-colored hair and lipstick to match. The look she gave him was, *just try to get my phone number, I dare you*, as if there were guys punching each other senseless trying to get to her. But that stare wasn't what bothered him the most. No, that would be the bone earring through her nose, which appeared in the dim light like silver-plated snot sticking out of either side. "No thanks, I'll pass," he mumbled to himself.

How about over here on the left? No, it looked like a table full of college-aged girls. As much as he would like to try it, he knew there was no way. They were too young and too fast for him. Besides, at that age, if he only used one of them for one night and then didn't spend any money on her, she would rat him out to his wife. No, he would leave them to their studies.

Over toward the right end of the bar, leaning up against it instead of sitting at a stool, was a prospect. She was blond and had a cute-looking face, a tight pink tee shirt, and ample hips coated by tight jeans. However, when she momentarily stood up straight, he could see that her body had an odd, compacted shape to it. To Max, she looked like a sexy Hobbit. *Hobbit sex*? No, that would be just a bit too weird.

It seemed like the rest of the customers were guys. As he was beginning to think it was just going to be a burger and a beer and then go home, he saw her. She was off to the left at the bar, waiting for a drink, looking as if she had just gotten there. She looked to be in her forties. Even in the dim light her platinum blond hair, probably from out of a bottle at a salon, stood out. She wore a white blouse and skirt that showed just enough of her crossed legs as she sat sideways on the barstool. She caught him looking at her. He didn't turn away, and she smiled. This one was out to have a good time, he could tell. He made his way toward the empty stool next to her.

With great confidence, he looked at her and asked, "Is anyone sitting here?"

"I guess you are now. Be my guest," she smiled pleasantly. Any wrinkles she might have had were well hidden by the low light. That was okay with Max. He wasn't planning on staying with her long enough for dawn to emerge anyway.

She turned toward the mirrored bar briefly, seeming to collect her thoughts for the next bit of dialogue. Max didn't let her turn away for long. "I'm, Max Bailer." He extended his hand. She took it without hesitation. Her touch felt a little colder to Max than he would have thought. Well, she had just come in from the cool evening also. *Besides, what's that they say, cold hands, warm what?* Well, he couldn't think of the exact wording at that moment.

"I'm Helen. Pleased to meet you, Max." "Helen. Helen what?"

"Just Helen—for now."

"Okay, Helen it is, then. So, are you having something to eat here tonight? I've never been here before. What's good on the menu?" He noticed that she was still smiling. That was good.

"Oh, I wouldn't know. This is my first time here, too. I haven't even seen the menu yet. The burgers sure smell good."

Before Max could answer, the burly, dark bear of a bartender butted in. Max hadn't even noticed him approaching from the other end of the bar. "They are good—the best in town. We take a lot of pride in them." Just like the bouncers, the guy had dazzling white teeth— very visible to Max through the curly, black vines that passed for the guy's facial hair. He passed small menus to both of them, but didn't really give either of them a chance to open them. "If you're daring enough, you might want to try our 'Express Burger.' We named it after the trains that come through out back. Hee hee!"

A chatty fellow, Max thought. Again, before Max or Helen could say anything, Mr. Bear, the Bartender, cut them off. "Can I get you something to drink first, a cocktail maybe? If I may, I would recommend the 'Flaming Choo Choo.'"

Max grinned and asked, "*The Flaming Choo Choo?*"

"Yes, it's our house favorite. It's a combination of a hot pepper infused vodka, a spritz of Tabasco, and a secret mixer to add just a bit more heat. We don't tell anyone what the mixer is because the drink is so popular here, other bars would copy it."

Max smiled at Helen, who was also grinning at the pudgy bartender who liked to talk a lot. "Well, Helen, are you up for some hot vodka tonight?"

"Sure, something hot tonight sounds good." She laughed loudly at herself.

Okay, my kind of woman, Max thought. "Alright my man, we'll take two of the Flaming Choo Choos, and, Helen, what about the special burger my man here talked about?"

She nodded.

"Okay, Mr. Bartender, we'll take the Express Burgers too."

Mr. Bear, the Bartender, beamed, "Sounds good, they come with slaw, instead of fries, it kind of takes some of the heat off. That okay with you?" He looked back and forth between them. They both nodded okay.

"Outstanding. Coming right up with those drinks, folks," and he trundled away to get them.

Max turned to Helen, "So, you come here often?"

126

She laughed, "No, Max, I told you this was my first time here. Are you not paying attention to what I'm saying?"

He grinned, "Oh, you're right, I forgot that. But I am paying attention. I'm just a little distracted, I guess, that's all."

"Oh, distracted by what?" She bit her lower lip and stared into his eyes.

"Well, it's certainly not the ambience of the place, that's for sure. It's nice to be sitting next to a pretty lady to distract me from the atmosphere."

He could almost see her blush through the dim light. "Well, thank you, Max, what a gentleman you are."

He couldn't respond before Bear the Bartender was back already with their drinks. It was a little annoying to Max that the guy was so quick and efficient. He hadn't had time to come up with a witty response to Helen. "You two enjoy the drinks. I know you will," he said. He flashed that high beam of a smile through his beard, and was off again down to the other end of the bar, splitting as quickly as he had gotten there.

The Flaming Choo Choos were served in those small mason jars that have become so popular at bars these days. They also came with what looked like a jalapeno slice floating at the top of each drink. Helen looked around at the other patrons—many, if not all, who seemed to be having this same drink. "My," she said, "don't these look fancy and popular. I guess they must be good."

Max nodded in agreement as he also noticed how many of the other customers were drinking the Flaming Choo Choo. He toasted Helen, the two of them clanked their mason jars together, and he said, "Well, here's to a hot drink, and hot times at a hot bar." She hesitated just for a moment, their eyes meeting over the top of the glass, and then she took a long sip.

"Whoa, that is hot!" she said, shaking her head in some disbelief. Max said nothing, but nodded in agreement, blowing breath out through his teeth.

Almost instantly though, she took another long sip. "Wow, it wouldn't take more than one of these to put me in a good mood."

Max asked, "A good mood for what, Helen?" as he gently rubbed his finger along her other hand that was resting on the bar over her purse.

She only smiled, and nodded side to side, wagging her finger at him. "Never mind, I still have to eat dinner, you know." They both took another swig of their drinks, going down easier now, as Mr. Bear the Bartender was back, and smiling as he set their food before them.

He said, "Enjoy the burgers, folks. Eat them like there's no tomorrow!" He laughed again at his own humor, and walked away.

The conversation had stopped between the two of them because the burgers, although spicy hot, were intoxicating—as if the meat, juices, and special sauce were aged and fermented together in some great kettle. They each had a forkful of the slaw to chase the heat of the burger. After several voracious bites of their food, Helen and Max stopped for a moment. She looked at him with excitement in her eyes. "This tastes fantastic! It's like an explosion of flavors in my mouth!"

Feeling buzzed from his drink, he might have made a vulgar comment to her in response to that, but right now he couldn't agree with her more about the burgers. "Lady, you are right about that. I don't know if I've ever tasted any burger so good! And the coleslaw is so different, too. It tastes, oh, I don't know, exotic, I guess. I'm not sure that I've ever tasted *anything* so good before. I've got to ask the bartender how they make these."

He looked down the bar toward Mr. Bear and called, "Hey, what's the recipe for. . ." But then he stopped in mid-sentence. Just like that, something wasn't right, something wasn't right in his stomach. He looked over at Helen and could tell that something wasn't right with her either.

He asked, "Does your stomach hurt?" Her slightly-raised hand and nod of her head told him yes. Mr. Bear seemed a mile away at the other end of the bar when Max tried to get his attention, but then he suddenly doubled over on his bar stool—his head almost landing in Helen's lap. *That feeling!* It was as if something was moving—something that felt scaly, insect-like. It squirmed, and then scurried around in there, gliding around the walls of his stomach. He had a vision in his head of some oversized centipede, each of its legs a burning matchstick, rampaging inside his belly, with fangs like white-hot darts biting into him.

He looked up in agony and saw Bear the Bartender, grinning at the two of them, taking away their plates. "I guess you two are done with these now. No one ever finishes them."

Helen was moaning next to him—also lurched over, holding her midsection, as if ready to wretch onto her pretty, white skirt. Max moaned, "What did you put in those?

The bartender held up a stubby finger. "Oh no, silence now, just watch this." Max wondered if those were claws instead of nails at the end of the bartender's fingers.

At that moment, the remainder of what had been their burgers leapt off the plates. Max only got a glimpse of the nasty centipede-like thing with yellow and red eyes as it flew past him onto the dirty floor. The two creatures landed at the same time, quickly scurrying away, on what looked like way too many legs. They crashed into the wood of the bar, and then just melted into it, blending into the structure. Max and Helen's horror showed in their wide-open mouths as they stared with bulging eyes at each other.

Suddenly, there was screaming, and the sound of plates and glasses crashing to the floor, and even tables being overturned. Turning in extreme pain, Max saw the bedlam that ensued. The customers, the Goth chick, the college girls, a muscle-bound biker, the sexy Hobbit, and all the others, were screaming in agony from their partially-eaten meals that had turned into nightmarish creatures. They were falling to the floor in disgust and pain— knocking over plates and utensils.

But there was something worse. It was the waitresses. They had changed. They weren't human anymore. Their clothes had ripped away as they morphed into screeching Harpies—sprouting wide bat-like wings. Wings flapping, knocking over more glasses and tables, they advanced, reaching down, digging talons into the hapless patrons writhing on the floor in agony. The screeching made Max's ears start to bleed. "GET UP! GET UP, DAMNED SWINE! GET IN LINE! GET READY TO MEET YOUR MASTER WHOM YOU WILL BOW DOWN TO! GET UP! GET UP!" They were forcefully pulled up off the ground, and herded over toward a back exit to the left of the bar.

Max and Helen were moaning in their own agony—their elbows and chins resting on the bar. Max could feel his physical body, his essence, beginning to wither away. The bartender stood in front of them. His features had darkened. The hair and beard were coarser—like bristles. The hands resting upon the bar were now fully-developed bear claws, and his eyes had turned yellow, demonic. But, worst of all to Max, when he opened his mouth to speak, all those teeth were gleaming white, and leonine.

His voice sounded to Max like raw sandpaper being scraped across his ears. "You are the accused, just as all who enter here are. But this is not the worst; this is merely a way station to your final destination. You will become subjects of the master and enter his realm of damnation. Are you ready?"

Helen managed to croak out, "But why? What have we done?"

Those yellow eyes blazed back and forth between the two of them. "Come now, Helen Bach, surely you must have known that this was your fate! Your poor husband—working two jobs to support your extravagant tastes—and how do you pay him back? By tramping around, like the dirty slut that you are and hooking up with the likes of Max, here.

"And you, Max Bailer! How many times have you done this to your poor wife, as she sits patiently with your two obedient children, just waiting for you to come home safely? You are as much of a filthy whore as this woman next to you is. The only difference between the two of you is that thing you've got hanging between your legs. You've

131

been using the wrong head to think with, Max, and now it's too late. It has cost you your soul."

"No, No!" Max moaned. Through all the pain and agony, on what was left of his wobbly legs, Max turned and tried to run for the door, past the screeching harpies, amidst the tumult of all the other lost souls in the bar. He made it as far as the door when he was grabbed from behind—deep claws digging into what was left of his shoulders. He heard, "Oh, no you don't, pig!" as he was twisted around and stared up into the hideous face of one of the bouncers.

The eyes were yellow, just like the bartender's, and the skin on its demonic bald head gleamed like black oil. When it spoke, it was a deep bass sound, but chopped, as if it were talking through a fan. And, just like the bartender, its teeth were those of a lion. With a sneer, it breathed fouling air down on Max. "Oh no, Max Bailer, all ye who enter here may never leave. Besides, you've still got one more stop to make!"

Max was whimpering, trying with whatever strength he had left to turn toward the door, but it was useless.

"You see, pig, our task is not to throw the unruly living out. We are here to keep the dead who are damned inside. However, I will afford you one more look upon the world outside before you leave for your final destination." With that, the demon twisted Max around and thrust his face against a greasy front window.

Max's eyesight was growing dim, but he saw clearly enough what was left of reality outside. He somehow understood each one's demise. Across the street, in a drugstore parking lot, the Goth chick lay sprawled outside the driver's side door of her car. It had something to do with consuming three cans of a highly-caffeinated energy drink, and a half pint of vodka. She had hoped the high dose of caffeine jetted into her bloodstream would allow the vodka to rush into her veins, giving her a quick buzz. It had worked. It had worked too well. She had made it inside the Tavern, but not physically.

The four college girls were slumped over in the front and back seats of a car in the Tavern's parking lot. They were victims of some strange suicide pact, brought on by overdosing on fentanyl. They had convinced themselves that this ultimate high would bring them to some higher plane of reality. Instead, it had brought them inside the Tavern to a lower plane of reality—a lot lower plane.

The muscular biker lay cold on the sidewalk— blood oozing around him from a fatal knife wound to the stomach, coming from a fight with a rival gang member.

Others that had been in the Tavern lay about in various death poses—with different degrees of carnage having caused their demise. These scenes were all separate, shrouded in mist, as if Max were looking at cartoon frames in a Sunday newspaper comic page. It was as if they had happened in various locations, most not even at the Tavern. But all these doomed souls had wound up at the Tavern, a place they had always wanted to visit, just like Max.

Just before the demon bouncer pulled him back from the window, one more frame materialized in the mist outside. This one, at least for Max, held the most horror of all. It was a scene of his car, smashed head-on in the parking lot with another car—the two front ends meshing together from the force of the impact. The violence of the collision drove him right over the airbag. Foolishly not wearing his seat belt, Max had smashed through the front windshield. His shredded skull and twisted body sprawled across the crumpled hood of his car. Across from him, on the rippled hood of her own car, as a result of the same foolishness, lay Helen Bach, a disorganized puzzle of bloody skull, head and hair, bones and viscera.

Ironically, one of each of their arms was stretched out, their hands touching. This was not "till death do us part." They were together forever now. At that moment, if he'd had a regular mouth and voice left, Max would have laughed at this dark, comedic repose. The demon bouncer pulled him away then, and shoved him toward the back exit, where the demon harpy waitresses were screeching, "GET IN LINE!" and herding the lost souls into a gauntlet—lining them up like pigs entering a slaughterhouse.

Helen, or the semblance of what used to be Helen's body, was herded in front of him. At this point, any clothes that were left on them had fallen away, or had been torn away from their frail, shrunken forms by the harpies. He looked at what was left of her back, and where her ass should have been. If her body had been shapely in life, it repulsed him now. The grey skin hanging from her shoulder blades rippled like waves eddying from a dead sea.

She turned her head to look back at his disgust. Dimming to blackness, small embers were all that were left of the eyes in her hollowed-out sockets. Her mouth had at one time been inviting, but now her rich, red lips had withered to a sickly pink—resembling a puckered anus, with its accompanying odor.

He had wanted so much to explore her breasts and the valley between them—even if they had been augmented. But now, they looked like small, featureless lumps, as if there were tumors festering under them.

As she saw the aversion in his eyes, he also saw the disgust with him in her own. His once firm chest and stomach were now a roiling ooze of pus-filled sores, which slimed down to his crotch. His once overactive member had withered away to a useless stub—the testicles falling off like small berries that had rotted on the vine.

Still, there seemed to be a moment of pity that they saw in each other, as the last of light began to fade from their eye sockets. Although they now knew that their mutual, illicit lust would never be consummated, there was a worse reason for despair. Where they were headed, there was intercourse, yes. In the tormented minds of their souls, they sensed it coming. Just as with all the other souls who enter there, male and female alike, they would be partnered to the same, single mate who burns for them. Each of the wretched dead will have to submit themselves to the cruel master. In their unholy coupling, they will burn with him, his limbs coiling around them, searing blasphemies into their damned souls. The expression "love hurts" does not apply in that realm of agony. There is no amount of pleasure to balance out the pain.

Suddenly, the back door of the bar blew open. "GET OUT NOW, SWINE!" the demon harpy waitresses screeched at them. Their line was forcefully shoved forward toward the darkness. In unison, both Max and Helen uttered, "Oh, God, no!"

The bartender, whose demonic features no longer resembled anything human, grated his voice on them. "Oh no, do not call upon Him now. You will not call upon Him ever again! Ye have a new master that ye shall serve!"

The line of withered souls was forced outside the bar, toward the railroad tracks where they waited. The demonic bouncers were front and back, the demon harpies flapped about them now on their wings, assuring that any who might try and flee, as if there were anywhere to go, would be corralled back to this spot.

The railroad tracks. Max noticed their real essence now for the first time. They weren't flattened rails of steel. They seemed to be alive, with a soft glow, pulsating, like a lava flow, but in a straight line. With what was left of his sense of sight, Max followed that line down to the right. The pulsating tracks seemed to simply end into utter blackness a short distance away.

Then he heard it and looked back to the left. The train was pulling into the station. He could hear the screeching of the wheels on those lava-like tracks, as it slowed to pick up its passengers. The pain of that sound was worse than the stabbing that came from the demonic insect that was inside of what used to be his stomach. Even as it slowed to a stop in front of the line of the damned, the terrible, painful noise did not end, and now Max saw why.

It wasn't screeching. It was a screaming sound. The wheels weren't made of metal that was forged in some netherworld factory. They were humanoid, skeletal souls, which had been impossibly twisted into circles, hands and feet fused together, and then coupled to the train. For these souls, their eternal punishment was to roll on the hell-bound tracks for all eternity—not as passengers, but as the actual wheels of the train, rolling in burning agony between its juggernaut weight and the searing heat of the molten tracks.

The train itself was just one big car—with no windows, no seams. It was just a mass of steaming blackness—like vulcanized rubber. Motion rippled through the structure, but with no purpose or direction. However, there was an inscription on the side. It had a name. The writing was ancient, symbols not letters, but Max and Helen, and all the others waiting in line for that last ride, were able to easily comprehend it, now that they were no longer alive. The train wasn't named something quaint, such as "Blue Comet," or "Silver Streak." It bore the name "Harlot of Babylon."

There was a splitting noise, like a burning tree falling in some forest fire, and an opening appeared toward the front of the train. The moaning and screams became greater, as they were all pushed inside by the gleeful demons. Helen turned and reached back with what was left of gnarled hands, trying to grasp onto Max, but one of the harpies wrenched her away. She let out a maddening howl as she fell into the train.

Max caught a glimpse of the end of the tracks before he was shoved in. A giant cauldron had appeared, pushed onto its side—wide and round enough for the mass of the train to drive into. Smoke and hellfire and horrid odors poured out from it. The colors of the flames were abominable, unlike any colors he had ever seen before. There were colors that weren't meant to be seen by mortal eyes, and odors that were conjured up from the depths of pure evil.

His last sane thoughts were of the life that could've been, regrets of the opportunities he had wasted, and the base human being that he had chosen to become instead. It could have been a life spent with a loving wife and children. It could have been a life of summers spent on sandy beaches, autumns laughing and thrashing about in a mixed palette of leaves with his children, winters dazzled by the pureness of snow and the warmth of a fireplace, and springs full of hope for the year that was to come. But he would never see their faces again. Then something else struck him. He would never see the face of God. That was the worst pain of all.

The train's opening seared shut behind him, and he joined all the souls thrashing about in their mutual dread. It rolled slowly forward toward the tortured kingdom that burned with agony and eternal damnation.

So, if you're ever driving down the road and come upon a "Last Stop Tavern and Grille" (there's more than one of them out there) with a fog-shrouded railway station behind it, and you're thinking of stopping in for a cold one, it's probably best to just keep moving on. Perhaps instead you should stop a little further down the road at the local church and roust the padre out of the rectory—hopefully to hear your confession. Maybe he'll even give you some real food and drink, like a consecrated host, and a sip of blessed, altar wine.

You see, back up the road at that Tavern and Grill with the train station behind it, they don't even serve cold ones. In fact, the drinks are always served way above room temperature. Nothing about the place is what it appears to be, but there are a few things that are certain. Besides the always fiery, wriggling burgers, and the sinister, liquid concoctions that go down like burning jet fuel, the train that pulls in is never late. It arrives often and, even though it's packed with riders, there's always room for one more.

If you Google the two words in the title of this story, you'll probably get a good idea of what it's about, even before you start reading. No matter, that won't spoil the ending. I'm sure you'll still find this tale to be a web of intrigue.

HOMO LYCOSIDAE

Something about this man attracted Harriet Olsen. It certainly could not be his looks. He wasn't what a woman would consider handsome. He was balding. He wore very thick eye glasses, which rested above a flat, pushed-in nose, and his lips were rather blubbery. Although his body seemed muscular, at about five, seven, he had a squat posture. For some reason, she also imagined him to be very hairy underneath his clothing—not just on his chest and stomach, but all over.

Not being a reservoir of confidence, Harriet certainly wouldn't brag to anyone else about her own looks. Her plain face supported glasses that were too obtrusive in front of brown eyes that appeared dull. Looking at her flat chest in the mirror, she would sadly muse that her nipples were like pimentos, but without the olives surrounding them. Her torso rested upon legs that were so spindly that she disliked wearing dresses for fear of showing off her too-lean thighs. She shied away from trying to enhance her appearance. Makeup was a mask to her. If a man would not like her for her true appearance, then he wasn't worth it.

She didn't exactly have a bunch of suitors banging down her door for a date. Therefore, she was smitten when Herman Carruthers, her professor of entomology at the college, invited her to his home to show her his personal collection of insect specimens. She probably should not have been surprised and should have seen it coming, due to him frequently calling on her in class for the answer. He would watch her intently as she would methodically describe the thorax and hind legs of a common grasshopper. With his eyes fixed on her very white throat, and his full-lipped smile, his face always showed approval when she would conclude her response.

But more importantly than their unfortunate looks, there was something else that they had in common. They both loved insects. Entomology was their passion. They loved to gaze at and observe the creatures. Studying their feeding, mating, and habitation seemed mind-boggling to Herman and Harriet. The thought that insects had so successfully fought back against man's onslaught of pesticides and emerged more resilient than ever could actually bring tears to Herman's eyes. The thought that they would probably one day outlast man and conquer the planet was calming to Harriet.

As a growing child, Harriet was never squeamish about handling insects—unlike many other little girls her age. The little boys who tried to scare her with them were disappointed. If she was handed a spider, an ant, or any other multi-legged little beast, she would eagerly accept it—as if being offered some glittering piece of jewelry to marvel at.

Herman once openly berated two students in a class for pulling the wings off a fly that had grown sluggish in flight. The two had managed to capture the creature in their cupped hands as it crawled across a desk. Carruthers came upon them as the now wingless fly sputtered and writhed— with the two knuckleheads laughing at its misery. The entire class stared in shocked silence at their professor's verbal onslaught. Harriet had thought to herself, *how could one man show so much compassion for this lowly, household pest?* Carruthers had noticed the staring students—especially Harriet—and composed himself, wiping the sweat from his brow as he continued class. He had made quite an impression on her with that tirade. The two knuckleheads dropped the class.

Such was the love of insects which fired both of their hearts, and which seemed to join them together as soul-mates. Harriett believed she had finally found a man to share a burning romance with. This was a man who would appreciate her for her knowledge and passion and was not concerned about her plain features. He would love her for her love of bugs. They would dance together like fireflies twinkling in a dusky meadow. She was sure of it.

However, she wasn't so blind as to think that her passion for insects was the only thing about her that he was attracted to. Despite her plain looks, she would sometimes catch him staring at her, as he paused in his lectures, and he would not immediately turn his gaze away. For those brief moments, he seemed to be examining her from the front of the classroom with the same intensity that he used on his six-legged specimens.

The thought of him now made her a little nervous, but at the same time excited. She had never slept with a man, but he would be hers tonight, she was sure—her first and, hopefully, her last. Before coming to class this morning, she had primped as never before, actually wearing a dress that stopped just above her knees—one she had found off the discount rack at a department store. It had black stripes that ran in a slanting pattern from top to bottom, strategically placed to hide her plain bodily features, as opposed to highlighting them. She believed it would create a little mystery to her body for the professor to explore. Her roommate was excited for her and had helped her pick out the dress.

That same roommate made sure that her mud-brown hair was freshly shampooed and combed as best as possible, to try and batten down any loose strands. She had tried to convince Harriet to get her nails done, but that was too much to ask. Harriet had been happy enough that her nails were at least clean, with none of the dirt that was so often embedded beneath them from her digging up grub and beetle specimens.

This man would show her tenderness. Harriet could feel it, and she was ready. It was a challenge paying attention in class this day, as she fidgeted in her chair. There was a delicious feeling of warmth in her thighs—something those limbs had never experienced before.

That feeling disappeared for the moment, as she thought about what her sister, Phyllis, had said to her. She attended the same college and was a year older than Harriet. But obtaining a college degree in landscape architecture was just a backup plan for Phyllis. Although she had somewhat of a curiosity about bugs, it was nothing to Harriet's extent. Her real passion was following their father's trade—masonry. In the same way that a collector of fine art would admire a Rembrandt or a Monet, Phyllis admired the way that masons and bricklayers could work with sand, stone, and mortar, and create functional sidewalks that curved, or construct buildings with spectacular angles.

Attending the same college, Phyllis was able to watch over her younger sister. Although Harriett knew she meant well, it sometimes felt as if she was overprotective, always wanting to know what was going on in her life, and if she had met anyone yet. Sometimes Harriett thought of her older sister as a gnat that keeps coming back, buzzing in your ear each time you try to swat it away.

Phyllis was that pestering way about Professor Carruthers. In their conversations, Harriett had confided to her older sister about her affection for the professor. But Phyllis did not care for Herman Carruthers. She had at one point referred to him as a lecherous pig. Phyllis told Harriet that, inside herself, she just felt that there was something wrong with the man. Harriett at first tried to brush off the comment by telling Phyllis that she was acting "buggy," chuckling at her choice of words. But her sister wasn't amused, and they had argued bitterly about Carruthers inviting Harriett over to his home. Phyllis kept on referring to it as his lair.

She had said, "I'm appalled that you would accept such an invitation from this man. I'm sure father would never approve if he knew."

"Oh, really? I find it ironic that you were always inquiring about whether I'd found a man to date in my life, and now that I have one, you want me to have nothing to do with him. And, as far as father is concerned, you were always his favorite. That's pretty obvious from the fact that he's providing the money for you to live in your own apartment off-campus." Brazenly, her voice rising with each word, Harriett finished, "I am a 21-year old woman, and I believe it's about time that I experienced a man, and neither you nor father can stop me!"

That exchange had occurred on the campus green the day before, and Harriett had not heard from, nor seen Phyllis since then. Harriett was now convinced that it hadn't been her plain looks, or her quiet manner, but

144

instead it was her sister's overbearing ways that were the reason she had not been dating. Well, that was going to change. She would copulate with this man whom she truly felt attracted to.

At 4:30 that afternoon, Harriett boldly climbed into the passenger seat next to Professor Carruthers. As the exhaust fumes spewed from the rear of his old, beat-up station wagon, and as he pulled away from the parking lot into the autumn afternoon, from across the parking lot, Phyllis Olsen raised her head above the dashboard of the Camaro she had borrowed from a classmate and fired up the engine. As they pulled out of the main entrance to the college onto the highway, she followed them, staying a couple of cars behind.

Carruthers began to speak as they rolled along. "You are going to love my collection, Harriett. I have many species of arachnids, Apis and Bombus, Dystera, Aedes, and others." Harriett, for her part, tried to keep up with his banter to impress him: *Yes, yes, very interesting, Professor, spiders, bees, both honey and bumble, flies and mosquitoes.* She was very nervous. *Show her his collection?* Is that all that was going to happen this afternoon at his home? She had other things on her mind, and stifled a giggle as she thought about him. She did not want him to think she was immature. She had to concentrate on what he was saying. For the rest of the ride she managed to keep a straight face and answer his questions about her fascination with mandibles, wings, antennae, and the like. It was like a pop quiz, for goodness sake!

Carruthers lived in a large home in a quiet part of the college town. Looking at the other houses on the block, they seemed to be set farther apart than other neighborhoods. Maybe they were a little too isolated from each other? She began to wonder if this was a good idea after all. *No, he's harmless and gentle, I just know it.*

It was an impressive house for a college professor. She was particularly intrigued by the back of the home that seemed to have a circular room attachment. Perhaps that was his exhibit room? She wondered how he could afford such a home, in such a neighborhood. However, he was the head of the entomology division within the college's biology department, so perhaps he made more money than his peers because of this? Perhaps he had inherited the home? It didn't matter to Harriett, it was his business, and she wouldn't pry into it.

As they pulled into the gravel driveway, Phyllis slipped the Camaro between some parked cars further down the street. Carruthers had shown no indication from the way he was driving that he knew they were being followed. Phyllis decided she would wait for a couple of hours to see if they would come out and if Carruthers would drive her back to her campus apartment. If Harriett didn't come out, she would find a way to break down the door. There was no way she was going to let her sister spend the night with this lecherous pig and let him defile her.

Inside, Carruthers had poured Harriett a glass of white wine. To her credit, despite turning 21 that year, she had not fallen into the trap of drinking too much as too many of her college peers did. However, she appreciated the wine at this moment. It had a calming, not yet giddy, effect on her. Then he led her into his laboratory. This was not yet the circular room that she had seen from the outside when they first pulled up to the house.

If the living room had been featureless, with its sparse furniture, the lab certainly was not. There was equipment everywhere. There were petri dishes, and gas jets, and bottles filled with various liquids and chemicals. Several long tables crowded the room. These were used for dissection of insects. All the trappings of a serious entomologist were present in the room.

Then of course, amidst all the books and paraphernalia, were the insects themselves. It seemed like hundreds, maybe thousands, of distinct species. They were split up into various terrariums, ant farms, and cages holding butterflies. Other specimens were preserved in small, glass display cases. The scene was a delight to Harriett. Here was an assassin bug consuming a cricket. Over there was a praying mantis consuming a small grasshopper. On one shelf mosquitoes and flies buzzed, trying to escape from their glassed-in environment. It was as if there was a whole universe of insects and bugs.

Carruthers called her over to a table. "These are my favorite specimens, Harriett, the arachnids, the spiders. As you know, they are not truly insects—obvious because of their eight legs instead of six—but those in the world outside of ours refer to them as insects. It is up to us entomologists, *and future entomologists*, to educate them." Looking directly at her when he said this, his lips parted slightly into his blubbery grin. Harriett was pleased that he had flattered her and returned a smile.

He removed the top from one of the terrariums, rolled up the sleeve of his lab coat, and placed his hand down in the glass case. He gently slid his fingers

147

underneath the hairy legs of a tarantula, one known as a "Tucson Blonde," and encouraged it to climb onto his palm. The creature complied. He lifted his palm out with the eight-legged creature clinging to it and offered it to Harriett. Without hesitation, she let the beast slide onto her own palm. As she did so, her finger tips momentarily touched those of Carruthers. Harriett gave him a brief glance, saw his grin, and turned her face bashfully away.

Recovering from that brief, hot flash, the spider comfortable in her left palm, she lowered her right index finger to pet the creature. Seeing the digit above, it raised its fangs to strike the intruding finger. Harriett stopped and gently lowered her finger onto the rear segment of the spider's body, stroking the fur, and never showing a moment of fear. The spider relaxed its fangs and was content to lay there and be caressed.

As Carruthers watched, a sliver of spittle developed on his lower lip. He admired the way she caressed the spider, and felt a bulge rise in his pants, and a tingling feeling in his crotch. He was thankful at that moment to be on the other side of the table from Harriett, his desire blocked from her view, for he did not yet want to give himself away. She looked up into his eyes, the desire in them somewhat clouded to her view because of his thick glasses. The Professor quickly sucked in his lower lip to consume the spittle before Harriett noticed. The sight of her standing there, caressing one of his favorite specimens with her gently-stroking fingers made him absolutely feverish. But he mustn't give himself away, not yet. He had to think of something quick to say.

"You know of course, Harriett, the only true tarantulas are of the European origin. The American species is technically a member of the Lycosidae family, the wolf spider."

"Y-yes . . . I knew that," she lied. She was concentrating on his bulging eyes behind those thick glasses. They looked both seductive and menacing to her. He wasn't leering at her, but seemed instead to be luring her with them. She stared down briefly at the hairy beast in her palm, ceased caressing it, and then stared again into the Professor's eyes.

"They are one of the few species that actually use sight to hunt their prey," Carruthers continued. As soon as the words were out, he knew it was the wrong thing to say. *Fool, look at her eyes, she is sensing that something is wrong!* He gently reached out with both hands and took the spider away from her and placed it back in the terrarium.

When his fingers touched her hands, she again felt that warmth in her thighs—despite his words about hunting prey echoing in her head, and that his eyes seemed to be growing darker behind the glass lenses. "Look behind you," Carruthers directed. She turned slowly and spied what he was talking about. On the desk behind them, in a small mesh cage, a male mantis was mounting a female.

Carruthers came up behind her and put his hands on her shoulders. She withered a bit under his grasp and breathed deeply. "Of course, Professor, she will consume her mate after they are finished copulating." At that, she quickly wheeled around and faced him. He was smiling slightly, and whatever menace had been on his face seemed to be gone for the moment. Her longing for him in that instant could not be denied.

With a look of dark innocence from behind those glasses he asked in a whisper, "You wouldn't do that to me, would you, Harriett?" She closed her eyes as his head bent forward and she let him kiss her. His thick lips parted hers as he slipped his tongue into her mouth. She felt a slight stickiness as their tongues met, not exactly the feeling that she was expecting. His tongue seemed to briefly attach to hers, as if by some epoxy. But when he pressed his pelvis and bulge against her, and drew her tightly into his arms, she was excited, despite the strange feeling between their tongues. Beneath her off-the-rack dress, her legs parted to draw him in.

Abruptly then, he pushed her away and glanced over to a door at the far side of the room. He turned back to her, his dark eyes seeming to smile behind the glasses, and said, "Follow me to the bedroom."

Carruthers took her by the hand and led her effortlessly towards the door. As she followed him into the darkness, and the door closed behind her, she never saw the tarantula that she had been caressing suddenly thrust itself against the glass walls of the terrarium. If it had a voice, perhaps it would have called out a warning.

The room was dark as midnight to Harriett. As she tried to walk forward, she stumbled and fell. The carpeting beneath her was amazingly thick. It was like walking on a giant sponge, sinking beneath her feet every time she tried to get up. She fell again onto her hands and knees. She rolled onto her back, pulling her knees up to try and sit up. The hem of her dress slipped up to her waist. "Herman, what kind of flooring is this?" That's when the light came on. Her parted, bare legs and underwear were exposed to him. Carruthers was able to stand, his naked body completely visible to her. His clothes had been discarded out the door.

150

The light was dim, but bright enough to see the surroundings. This didn't look like a bedroom to her. There was no bed, no furniture, only one cheap-looking lamp plugged into the far wall. The whole flooring seemed to sag. Actually, it rippled. It was a velvety fiber, probably quite expensive. It felt as if there was water underneath, to account for the rippling effect. The lamp had a wide, round base to support it so that it wouldn't flip over from all the swaying and rippling. Harriett began to think that this surface wasn't designed for walking. It seemed designed instead for making escape difficult.

Carruthers was excited. It was obvious from his erection, which had an odd shape and curvature that she had not expected to see. He was also drooling. Feeling embarrassed, but more frightened, Harriett pulled her knees together to try and conceal herself from him. "The floor is designed like a spider's web," Carruthers explained. "It is supposed to be soft and spongy, difficult for insects to walk on. It is not sticky silk, as most human dregs believe." It then struck Harriett, despite the priapic growth between his legs, that her professor wasn't really interested in her for sex.

"But what do you want . . . .?" she stopped abruptly. His glasses were off. As she had fantasized when getting ready for their rendezvous, he had hair all over his body, but as she watched, it was growing. It was the eyebrows that she noticed first—becoming blacker and thicker, as though she was watching through a sped-up time-lapsed view. Then she noticed the rest of his body becoming matted, and his frame seemed to be squatting closer to the spongy floor every moment.

Seconds later, he was belly down to the floor, which rippled as he assumed that position. She could see that his back and rear were now covered with thick bristles. He momentarily lowered his face. Suddenly, he raised his head to look at her. She wanted to scream for help, but the words dried up in her throat. His head had bulged and become elongated, and there were two smaller eyes now staring at her above the bulging, black orbs that had replaced his original set.

As he began speaking again, a fifth and sixth eye burst forth from his now bristle-covered face, just above and to either side of the third and fourth. The speech coming from him was garbled, as if he was choking on it. "Lycanthropy . . . It is not something . . . related . . . only . . . . to wolves . . . as mo-ost . . . humans . . . th-think. It . . . applies . . . to any . . . shape shifting."

Now his rear end was extending from the rest of his torso, and his body became segmented. His arms and legs became spindly, black appendages, covered with those same bristles. Four stumps, two on each side, suddenly cracked through his skin. They extended out between each arm and leg. Segmented, they became legs themselves. He now had eight of them.

Harriett still had not moved. It wasn't just the paralysis from fear; she also couldn't help being fascinated at what she was witnessing. Gazing from his legs up into his six eyes, the voids staring into her, his words from before scurried around in her mind: *they are one of the few species that actually hunts its prey by sight.* Arachnid. Lycosidae. Wolf spider. Lycanthropy. The reality of the giant were-spider looming before her finally hit home like a hammer, and she let out a scream.

"Roo . . . oom . . . sound . . . proo . . . ofed," sputtered out of the were-spider's mouth.

Harriet finally moved, trying to slide along on her rear, still facing the Carruthers-Spider thing. But the skill with which he had constructed his man-made web hampered her efforts. She realized then that this was the circular back room she had seen from the street. Her right hand suddenly grasped what she thought was a rock. In the dim light of the room she hadn't noticed other objects behind her. It tipped over from her grasp, and she fell back onto the spongy carpet. Turning her head to the right, she cried out in disgust at what she saw. It wasn't a rock in her hand, but instead a human skull, clean and dry. The rib cage next to it still had some tattered flesh clinging to various parts of the bones.

With strength propelled by fear, she rose up, and in the same motion hurled the skull at the Carruthers-Spider's head. He swiveled his head to the left, and the skull struck the wall behind him, breaking it into pieces of bone and teeth.

What had been Carruthers now reared up on its eight spider legs. Next, there was a scraping, grinding sound—as of bones crunching against each other. His jaw dropped lower, and his lips split apart, as two, narrow, serrated fangs suddenly protruded through the blood and spittle frothing from his mouth. They slid out about a foot and then stopped. There was some kind of bloody fluid dripping from their tips.

Harriett managed to scramble on the surface until her back was against the rear wall. The shock, the thought of impending death, paralyzed her again. The insect world is a cold, cruel one, she thought to herself, seeing her reflection in the were-spider's six eyes. She suddenly hated insects with all of her heart.

The next second, he pounced upon her. It took only two leaps for him to cover the great distance across the room. His shadow looming over her, and his legs gathering her in, he raised his head to strike. He wasn't completely transformed into a spider. His forehead protruded out, not covered with bristles, and his ears were still there, though covered in the thick hair.

Harriett, with tear-stained cheeks, looked into his original eyes. Through her tears they were like shimmering black pearls. She whimpered, "Her-man . . . I loved you . . . I . . . thought you loved me?"

The Carruthers-Spider's head cocked to one side slightly, hesitating, as if contemplating what she had said. *Pity this poor human female, it thought for a second. But then, this is so much more merciful than say, pulling the wings off a fly.*

Then it struck down at her, the fangs piercing her vulnerable throat, and lodging in her spinal cord. Her arms flailed back against the wall, and she made a gurgling sound, but it did not last long. The poison from his fangs seeping inside her quickly numbed her into unconsciousness. His lower jaw was now a jagged, sharp mandible that ripped through the fabric of her dress and snapped her bra in the front. It tore through the flesh between her breasts, lodging onto her ribcage for better purchase as the were-spider sucked her essence out of her. She felt none of this, for her nervous system was now completely deadened by the poison.

He backpedaled on his eight legs toward a more comfortable position on the bouncy fabric. Squatting down on his legs, he delighted in his feast. Her life fluids were drained from every source in her reservoir. When he was done, her muscle and fat would be gone, leaving just her dried skin clinging to her skeletal frame as peeling, rotted wallpaper might cling to sheetrock.

As he sucked out the last of her tributaries, he heard a crash of breaking glass from his laboratory. Somehow, one of the terrariums must have gotten knocked over. Specimens would escape. His precious children! His wards! He dropped the remains of Harriett and turned to leap for the door to his lair when it suddenly burst open. Standing there was a strange woman whom Carruthers, in his human mind did not at first recognize. He was temporarily still, amazed at the intruder. Who would dare to penetrate his lair? How did it get in?

Phyllis Olsen stared in ghastly wonder at the remains of her sister. She knew it was her. Although, the shrunken head was unrecognizable, the tattered remains of her off-the-rack dress were still very visible. She had waited outside until she could stand it no longer, and then had broken in—vowing to steal her sister away from Carruthers' arms if she had to. But she was too late. She stared at Harriett's remains with a growing sorrow. Moving her eyes to the were-spider, the sorrow began to turn to hatred. The creature seemed to be grinning—as bits of her sister's flesh hung from its fangs.

"A . . . second . . . meal," it choked out.

Her eyes raging with tears, Phyllis screamed, "Look what you've done to my sister! I tried to tell her. I tried to warn her about you. I could feel it inside me that there was something wrong with you, but she wouldn't listen. Foul arachnid! Filthy, eight-legged spore! You will pay horribly for this!"

If the Carruthers-Spider was still amused, it was only momentarily. Now there was something familiar about this human dreg. He recognized her from somewhere. On campus, that was it! He'd seen her on campus. But still, it seemed he'd seen her somewhere else.

Phyllis's tears were starting to dry and were replaced with a cold, brutal look at the were-spider. "I see, spider scum, that despite all these species you have in your lab, a particular one is missing. There is at least one insect missing," she said.

The were-spider had been getting ready up on its legs to pounce, but it paused at her words. It cocked its head again, as if puzzled.

"No wasps?" Phyllis asked. Carruthers's arachnid senses picked up a strange quality seeping into her voice. It was like a low hum, or a buzz, as if she were talking into a fan. "No Sceliphron, no mud dauber wasps?" she continued. "They paralyze you with their sting, and then feed you to their young, don't they?"

Her voice was definitely humming now, as if there were a hornet's nest next to his ear. The Carruthers-Spider was suddenly frightened. Now he remembered where he'd seen the sister before. It was at a lecture for a group of enthusiasts of para-science, a lecture on lycanthropy. His own words to Harriett came back to him: *Lycanthropy is not something only related to wolves, it applies to any shape-shifting.* Something had come into his web— something that would not be seized and consumed. This creature came for him. Slowly, his eight legs moved away from the remnants of Harriett.

Phyllis Olsen grinned at the Carruthers-Spider. Her eyes suddenly bulged to five times their normal size in her expanding head. They were the multi-faceted eyes of a wasp. She saw a hundred images of the Carruthers-Spider and sensed its fear. She spoke calmly with the hum in her voice. "You see, our father knew about my…tendencies. We both thought it best that Harriett not be told about my secret. The only thing Harriett ever thought strange about me was my love of working with cement, as father does. But father also believed I could use my abilities to keep an eye on my little sister and keep her safe, and he instructed me to do so."

She stripped off her own light dress, wearing nothing underneath—a naked, human female from her neck down, but not for long. "Father will be displeased with me for failing. He will be angry that you have attacked our hive. But he will be comforted knowing that I have found a source for my progeny, and my descendants, to live on."

At that point, she metamorphosed. Her neck, torso, arms and legs changed, and the long, skinny, segmented body of a giant wasp was there. She had become a mud dauber wasp—a species that uses dirt and secretions to form solid mud nests, just as a human would mix materials to make concrete. The Mud Dauber—nature's mason. Her delicate wings quickly protruded out and began beating, making the spider's lair hum and vibrate. Her head was no longer there. Instead it was eyes and antennae, and a large v-shaped mouth.

The Carruthers-Spider knew it was facing its worst enemy, and it had come into his own abode. He stared in fear at the Olsen-Wasp's body. Mostly, his six eyes scanned down the length of the thin stem that connected the front section to the rear section. There, at the anus, was the stinger. It continuously slipped in and out, as if it were a poison-loaded piston.

He knew he couldn't get past the Olsen-Wasp. His only hope was to fight it off. He rushed at her, but in this confrontation in nature, the spider, trying to overpower the mud dauber, always loses.

However, instead of meeting the attacker head-on, the Olsen-Wasp easily lifted itself from the spongy fabric of the floor on its fine wings. The Carruthers-Spider saw the opportunity, and raced underneath, trying to escape through the door. Instantly, she dropped back down on the were-spider's bristle-covered back—straddling it with her legs. It was a human scream that came out as her stinger was brought down again and again on the giant arachnid. It did not take long for him to become paralyzed from the poison injected into his body. As he had done to Harriett, so it was done to him.

With the were-spider now powerless, the were-wasp dragged the creature out through the doorway into the lab. In the terrarium, the Tucson Blonde tarantula seemed to cower in a corner of its glass home, fearful of the giant, humming wasp, and what it had done to the master.

Although essentially comatose, the Carruthers-Spider could still see blearily through its six eyes. There was a broken window into the lab. It was made of thick glass and would have taken tremendous power to break through. Apparently, even in human form, her strength was commensurate to that of her wasp form. *Of course*, it was the window glass breaking that he had heard, not a terrarium crashing to the ground. She had said that there was something suspicious about him. If she suspected his lycanthrope abilities she knew that, with him having a lair, he would have no alarm system set up with the local police. Why would he ever want to summon the police here to find this? *Clever were-wasp,* he thought, no one was coming to the house to check and see if there might be trouble.

He didn't have long to dwell on this. Suddenly, her wings began to vibrate faster as she still straddled him, and then she seemed to emit a screeching, buzzing sound from her mouth. An instant later, wasps swarmed in through the broken window and around him. They were mud daubers, just like her.

The finality of the horror set in to what was left of his human-arachnid brain. Not only had she impregnated him with her own spawn, but now her insect-sized sisterhood would use him as an incubator for their young as well.

He didn't feel pain anymore; he just felt the prodding and poking of a thousand tiny stingers as the Olsen-Wasp stood guard over him. He wouldn't die—not yet. No, that would come after the hatching, when the young larvae would eat their way out of him for nourishment to adulthood. If he could feel nauseated, he would. But there was nothing physical he could do. His brain would just go over and over the terror that was happening to him until they finally ate into it.

In the terrarium on the table, the senses of the Tucson Blonde tarantula were on overload as its six eyes took in the whole scene. Instinctively, it flopped over onto its back, numb with fear. It played dead, hoping that it would not experience the same fate as its master.

For a number of years while our kids were growing up we used to vacation with other family members every summer on North Carolina's Outer Banks and Hatteras Island. There are all kinds of stories on the Banks about shipwrecks and ghosts, and pirates and ghosts and dark, stormy winds and ghosts. Did I mention there are a lot of stories about ghosts? Yeah well, this is my particular spin on those stories. Additionally, the waters around the Banks and Hatteras can be rough, unpredictable, and violent—a perfect backdrop to stir the imagination into concocting weird stories. I've drafted several so far that may appear in a future collection of tales that all take place on the Banks. Stay tuned. Hey, how's that for a little bit of shameless self-promotion, huh?

AVON'S SEA GHOST

Ten Years Earlier

"This always happens when you drink, Lionel! It's what's causing all the problems we've been having! Look, you haven't even noticed that you cut yourself with the knife!" Mary Whalen punctuated the shouting at her husband with a lot of pointing of her fingers and thrashing about of her arms. When the evening started, she had looked forward to a romantic night out for dinner, and then possibly a fun romp in bed for dessert. However, the night had now deteriorated into this vocal, drunken loathing.

Among his colleagues, Lionel had a reputation for being nasty when he drank, and Mary could attest to that. This particular night, she had also had a few, thinking she was entitled to it, since Lionel was doing the driving. Her fuming began on the way home from the restaurant when he had the audacity to question her about how much *she* had drunk, as she warily watched him trying to keep the rental car in the correct lane.

Actually, Lionel *had* noticed that he gave himself a cut on the thumb when slicing the lime for her vodka, but he was trying to hide it, knowing she would make a big deal out of it. After all, he didn't think it was bleeding that badly. It was no cause for alarm as far as he was concerned.

Still ignoring her remark about the knife, he shot back, "I don't drink too much! Considering that I have to put up with you, I probably drink too little!" He turned to the wet bar he was leaning against and grabbed the bottle of

Scotch, then struggled to get ice from the bucket to his glass.

The Wall Street broker and his glitzy wife had found the house through a real estate agent and were renting it for a week. The house was on the beach at Avon, one of the little towns that are scattered along the beaches of the Outer Banks on the way to Hatteras Village. The beaches on Long Island and the Jersey shore were too crowded anymore and had too many regulations for his liking. Over initial objections to visiting an area unfamiliar to them, Lionel had convinced Mary that a week away from their City life in a quieter, less commercial place, such as the Banks, would be just what their ailing marriage might need.

He thought things had gone pretty well the first night; they had even slept together in the same bed. But the quiet time got old for them pretty quickly. Despite its rough waters, the Outer Banks proved too calm for a couple used to living and working in New York City, where life travels at the speed of light, and where they were a healthy distance from each other during most of the work week. Within a few days of lying around and sunning on the beach, they were getting on each other's nerves. Prior to this night, Lionel had actually moderated his drinking on this vacation. However, waiting for their table at the bar, he had taken full advantage of the two for one happy hour. Mary probably had one less round than him, but who was counting? Lionel knew that in the hands, stomach, and then the brains of the wrong people, alcohol becomes an uncouth third party crashing a dinner date. *But that analogy didn't apply to them, of course.* With one in each hand, as if on a lazy, hazy river, the drinks had floated them over to their dinner table.

The worst result of all that imbibing, Lionel now realized, was that their neighbors, also renters, could probably hear them arguing through the open windows. The breezes on the Banks carry sound pretty well.

Mary watched in frustration as Lionel poured himself another drink. She slurred at him, "You see, you see! That's exactly what I'm talking about!" When he turned from the bar to respond, emboldened by her own intake of drunkard's fuel, she hurled her vodka and tonic across the room—the liquid flying all over the floor before the tumbler hit him square in the chest. An amazing shot, considering she was so tipsy.

Lionel's mouth gaped open, and he bellowed, "Stupid, drunken bitch!" He lunged at her, but was surprised when she didn't retreat, and rushed forward right at him instead. When they met, she lashed out at him with her right hand, but he caught her arm and then grabbed the other, throwing her down in front of the open glass and screen doors that led out to the deck facing the sea. Her yellow cocktail dress fluttered about her as she landed on the floor. He had opened the screen doors because, even though she was annoyed with him, she had agreed to sit out on the deck to hopefully enjoy the night breezes. However, when he decided to have another drink, he knew by her reaction all that would be left of the evening was for the argument to escalate to its current point.

Mary was struggling to get to her feet. She finally stood up, but stopped herself. Lionel also stopped moving. A white glow began to envelope the room. For an instant, Lionel marveled at how it highlighted the patterns in

Mary's dress. When she first began screaming at the luminescence surrounding her, Lionel simply stood drunk and dumbfounded. In the midst of the white, there was something red. It looked like some beautiful, crimson flower that was poisonous to the touch.

Mary's continued screams finally jolted him to action. He scanned about frantically, looking for some kind of weapon. The knife that he had used to cut the lime was on the wet bar. Her screaming died in his ears as he raced to grab the knife, and when he turned she was gone. A pool of her blood coated the small throw rug by the open doors.

"Mary! Mary!" he howled as he ran forward. He slipped when the bloody throw rug went out from under him, and he smacked his head on the floor. The alcohol assured that he was knocked out.

At daybreak, he was awakened from his unconsciousness by the police banging on, and then banging down, the door to the rental. They found him lying there, Mary's blood congealed to the rug, and the knife still in his hands. He kept blubbering to them that some great, white phantom had taken away his precious, beloved Mary.

And there was born the legend of the Sea Ghost of Avon.

Present Day

"So, the place is supposed to be haunted, huh?" Devon McCabe asked. There were seven of them altogether. They were sitting around a bonfire on a blanket on Avon beach, drinking and smoking, and playing around on their smart phones, running up roaming charges on their parents' accounts. It was a week before "in season," the last full week of June. The next week would lead into the 4th of July and the beaches and rentals would be more crowded. This night, there were only three or four fires burning up and down the beach. Devon's group was the closest to the house that Lionel and Mary Whalen had rented 10 years earlier. It was about 100 yards south of their bonfire. They were all looking in that direction now, discussing the events and the lore surrounding the house.

There were three couples, college students that had met at N.C. State and had become friends. There were Devon, and Sookie Wheldon, Bryan Littleton, and his girlfriend, Mandy Soyers, who had already been dating back at school, and Joe Wolchewicz, and Tara Mailer, who had started dating when they started work that summer.

Devon had addressed the question to the seventh among them, Billy Joe Maynard, manager of a local restaurant with an Australian theme called the "Down Under," and a local who had been raised in Manteo up in Currituck County. He'd gone away to Syracuse on a basketball scholarship, but when college was over and it was apparent that he wasn't going to the NBA, he got tired of the cold in upstate New York and returned to the Outer Banks. He had worked in the restaurant business for several years before he landed the manager's job about five years ago. Two of the couples present he had hired for the summer to bartend and wait tables. He had ten years on all of them, more experience and wisdom, but despite having a college degree, he suspected that the Yankee kids just thought of him as some uneducated yokel, who never really made it out of the South, so he wasn't too interested in hanging out with the hired help when they had asked him to join them tonight.

165

On the other hand, he was single, and didn't have anything else planned, so he agreed to go out to the beach tonight to have a few beers with the youngsters. It had been awhile since he'd had a steady girl in his life, and he thought that this Sookie might be worth testing. She'd stopped into the restaurant a few times to meet with the others, and he knew that she worked with Devon in one of the surf shops that dot Highway 12 up and down the Banks. Back in his college days, especially playing on the basketball team, he'd met his share of young ladies who were fascinated by his southern accent, and who didn't mind experimenting in bed. Something about the way Sookie dressed, and because of some of the strange conversations he'd overheard her have in the restaurant, made him think that she might be interested in a guy who was a few years older. By the time he started his third beer, though, it became apparent that she was more interested in Devon, and that the other college kids just wanted to hear the legend about the haunted beach house from the local guy.

It was senior year for all of them. They were from Cape Cod and other points up north—except for Sookie, who was actually from Raleigh. Billy Joe suspected that they had convinced their mommies and daddies to let them stay in North Carolina and work, instead of coming home for the summer. They probably convinced their parents that this would be a way for them to get more experience at doing things on their own, such as doing laundry and the dishes, hopefully not all together in the sink or washing machine. Of course, mommy and daddy probably paid their rent. That freed up the funds from their summer jobs for more important things, such as beer, cheese fries, and birth control. He wasn't exactly in the mood to entertain them with local legends, just so they could then go off and ridicule the local people for believing in such things.

"So, what about it, Billy Joe, is the place haunted? What's the story behind it?" Devon asked again.

"Well, I don't know if you guys really want to hear the story. It's just local island stuff."

But they all chimed in between sips of their beer, "Oh come on, of course we want to hear." Billy Joe noticed that the one couple, Bryan and Mandy, were really starting to get drunk, repeating their words, and rubbing each other's thighs, as they sat on the blanket, with no regard as to who was watching.

"Yeah, come on Billy Joe," Devon said, "It's what we do during a bonfire."

"Please, Billy Joe, I'd really like to hear about it." It was Sookie. He looked at her for a moment. She looked past him to the house, and then back into his eyes again. She wasn't drinking as much as the others and seemed more sincere about hearing the story than they did. Being from Carolina herself, she would probably be less likely to mock the locals than the northern kids would.

"Well, it started about 10 years ago." They all sat up a bit and tried to pay attention, especially Sookie. Even Bryan and Mandy stopped groping each other for the moment.

"Most of you, being from the North," he glanced again briefly at Sookie, the lone exception, "might've heard of this guy, Lionel Whalen, and his wife, Mary, who came down from Manhattan and rented the place for a vacation. He was a successful Wall Street type who murdered his wife there in a drunken rage, or so they say."

"Me and Joe are from Cape Cod and Connecticut. We wouldn't know so much about some dumb ass stockbroker from New York," Devon piped in. He and Joe chuckled at that. Billy Joe stared at him for a moment. He didn't like this kid from Cape Cod—a stuck up New Englander, as far as he was concerned. Or was it because Sookie was sitting so close to the uppity punk?

Sookie gave Devon a brief, annoyed look. "Go ahead, Billy Joe. 'Or so they say.' What did you mean by that?" She was looking very intently at him.

He continued, "Well, between Manteo and the Banks, I've lived most of my life around here. Know a lot of the people, including a lot of the cops." He took a sip of beer. "A cop buddy of mine was telling me about the case over a couple of drinks one night, awhile back. He said that the other rich tourists in the surrounding houses could hear a loud argument coming through the open windows. Some of them admitted to the cops that they heard the wife screaming for help at one point. But hell, they were on vacation, only had one week to escape the rat race, and they weren't going to get involved in this drunken couple's domestic fight. They were just satisfied when the argument seemed to be over.

"Well, early the next day, one of these visitors remembers the screams from the night before and, I guess feeling a twinge of guilt, decides he'd better call the cops."

Of all of them, Billy Joe could see that he had Sookie's attention most of all. She absent-mindedly worked one arm around Devon's. He didn't remove it.

"Well, the cops busted down the door. They found Lionel passed out in a pool of his wife's blood—with a knife in his hand. It seemed obvious to them that he had murdered his wife, and then probably dumped her body in the water. Afterwards, though, in his drunkenness, he must have come back into the house and passed out without having cleaned up any of the blood."

"So, what's the ghost story about?" Devon asked.

Billy Joe went on, "I'm getting to that. As they're taking Lionel away, all hung over and hysterical, he's babbling that 'a ghost came and snatched his wife away.'"

"Yeah, right," Devon chuckled. He got up and stumbled over to the cooler for another beer. He plopped himself back down next to Sookie, who sat cross-legged on the blanket. As he sat down, without looking at her, his hand landed on her right thigh. She didn't push it away when it lingered there for a moment longer before he pulled it away.

That didn't go unnoticed by Billy Joe as he continued. He glared at Devon, and then turned to the others. "So, anyway, for days afterward, Lionel kept babbling about this white ghost that came and took away his beloved Mary. The Dare County D.A., of course, wasn't buying it and wanted Lionel tried for murder. But his family up north obviously had a lot of money and got involved. Lionel seemed to be going nuts from this thing. Eventually, the family got a psychiatric examination done, and he was determined to be insane. With his brain probably fried from alcohol, he couldn't go to trial.

"The family got him moved back up to New York to an institution up there, and folks around here never saw him again. Because of what happened in that house, though, the story that the place is haunted has lived on."

Devon wasn't paying too much attention anymore. He kept glancing over at Sookie with a buzzed grin on his face. She would return the glance every now and then.

"Why does it live on? What do the locals think, Billy Joe?" Tara asked. She and Joe were still listening.

Billy Joe had noticed that Bryan and Mandy were lying back down on the blanket, giggling because they had spilled a beer. "What?" He had turned away from them and was looking at Devon and Sookie together. "Oh yes, well, some people say they hear howling or moaning coming out of the place, sometimes even in the daytime. Some believe it's the ghost of Mary herself, coming back to get revenge on Lionel. But, you know, there are shipwrecks up and down these shores. Everyone knows about the pirates that frequented here."

"What are you talking about?" Devon asked.

"Well, there are a lot of superstitious folks living on the Banks. There are tales of mutated, scary cats down on Ocracoke, haunted lighthouses, things like that. A lot of folks think the ghosts of the pirates roam the shores of the Banks. Some people think that the ghost of Blackbeard, or Steade Bonnet, or Calico Jack Rackham, or one of the others got Mary, and that's what drove Lionel insane."

"Is that why the place is so run down now? Do people think it's haunted and are afraid to go there?" Sookie asked.

Billy Joe gave her a faint smile. "Well, it got a reputation after the murder. The realtors had a hard time getting anyone to rent the place. Even the tourists from up north, who didn't believe in ghosts, weren't too thrilled about renting a place where a brutal murder was said to have been committed. It was just too creepy. After awhile,

170

it seemed like the realtors didn't try very hard to rent it, and the place has deteriorated from neglect through the years. It should probably just be torn down."

"Anything else we should know?" Devon asked with his stupid grin. He then laid back on the blanket, trying to get closer to Sookie, who wasn't keeping her distance.

Billy Joe was pissed off at this spoiled Yankee brat. He glanced at Sookie and looked at Devon lying there. "Not quite done. They say that some foolish tourists go exploring the place every once in awhile, and then never come back."

Devon got up, leaning on his elbows, staring at him. Billy Joe held his gaze for a second and glanced at Sookie, then leaned back a little on the blanket himself, and grinned, "'Course, these are just rumors. Nothing substantiated."

Devon pressed him, "And what do you think, Billy Joe?"

Trying to make me look like a fool, huh boy? Good thing this kid didn't work for him at the restaurant. He'd fire his Cape Cod ass in a minute. "You tell me, Devon. You're a college boy. Surely you've read some Shakespeare?"

"And?" Devon sat up, bold from the beer, and not missing the insult. Sookie gripped his arm.

"*And*, Ole Willie said something once like, 'There are more things in heaven and earth then you can imagine.' Something like that. Well, son, there probably *are* more things than *you* can imagine."

Devon began snickering. Joe and Tara chuckled a little bit too. Bryan and Mandy were lying on the blanket and just couldn't wait any longer—groping each other as best they could with everyone around them.

Billy Joe swigged the rest of his beer and stood up, telling everyone he had to leave. "I've got to open up the restaurant early." He looked at the four that worked for him. "You guys don't have to come in until later, so you can hang around drinking some more. I can't."

"Aww, come on, Billy Joe, don't go!" Devon chided.

"No, thanks for the beers, I've got to go. See you guys tomorrow." He looked briefly at Sookie. She returned a look that seemed to say she was sorry for the way he was treated. Then he turned and started walking up the beach. *Stupid Bohemian chick,* he thought to himself. *If she wants that Cape Cod asshole, let her have him.* Moving away from them, he muttered to himself, "I hope they both go for a swim and get eaten by sharks."

Sookie briefly watched him walk away. The two groping each other hadn't even acknowledged Billy Joe leaving. At this point, they had their hands up each other's shirt. Mandy was starting to make some slight cooing sounds. The others began snickering. The moment was already awkward enough with the exchange between Devon and Billy Joe. The college lust now happening before them made it even more so.

"Uh, I think we're going to take a walk up the beach and then head back home. Leave these two to the rest of the beer, and other things," Joe said.

"Yeah, I think so," Tara laughed, and agreed. They got up to leave.

It looked like Devon was about to suggest that he and Sookie head home also, but she interrupted him, "C'mon, Cape Cod. Let's go for a walk." She grabbed him by his hand and pulled him to his feet, then began leading him away in the other direction, toward the house down the beach.

Tara and Joe both smiled at them. Sookie continued pulling on Devon's hand. "Have fun you two, stay away from the haunted house," Joe hollered.

Devon turned briefly and gave them a thumbs up. "See you, bro'," he replied to Joe, and then let himself be led away.

They hadn't really hung out together at N.C. State, but had met one another through the other four, and then shared a class together. Sookie's dad knew some of the folks who ran businesses down along the Banks and had gotten her the job at the "Surf Shop."Although the water was obviously colder up north, she found out that Devon had learned to surf during summers at Cape Cod and Martha's Vineyard. She got him in at the Surf Shop also. They both preferred working there, rather than serving beer and hush puppies to crusty, local party boat captains.

Sookie wasn't her real name. It was actually Mariah. At one time, someone had told her that Sookie stood for some kind of flower, but that was really of no significance to her. She'd heard it in a song from the sixties, and simply liked the sound of it. She preferred that everyone call her that.

Her dad was manager at a branch of East Carolina Bank in Raleigh. He'd flirted with a hippie lifestyle himself at one time while attending Duke. He was still in touch with an old college buddy who had never given up that lifestyle, and who ran the surf shop in Avon, thereby getting Sookie the job for the summer.

Sookie knew that, after he had finished college, her dad came to realize he preferred making money to attending rock concerts and smoking weed. Her two older sisters shared his monetary interest, but she was always fascinated by his stories, and the music of the sixties and seventies. To obvious dismay, she was adopting that lifestyle, as evidenced by her choice of nicknames, and the clothes that she wore. Tonight, for instance, she was wearing a long skirt on the beach that looked like burlap, with a tie-dye tee shirt and matching purse. Her father had seen the outfit once before and had remarked that she looked like a Joan Baez wannabe.

However, her mother had persuaded her father that, instead of forcing her to work at the bank between semesters, perhaps working at the beach for the summer, and not making much money, would show her the value of earning a buck. Her father fell for that ruse. For Sookie, the part about learning to love money hadn't sunk in yet.

At this moment, Sookie didn't quite understand why she was attracted to this guy, Devon. As with her father, if he wasn't into money now, he would be some day. That was the Cape "Cod-ness" in him. He wasn't exactly her type. Besides which, he could be rude, especially when drinking. She hadn't liked the way he had treated Billy Joe tonight.

Still, as they had gotten to know each other better, her attraction to him had grown. Maybe it was the way that Cape Cod spilled from his tongue as "CapeCad." That New

England accent sounded so quaint. Perhaps because he was a surfer, he would like the sixties?

Surely, it couldn't be his eyes? She'd once overheard a girl in class whisper to another one about his eyes. *Silly, smitten cows, they were. She wasn't one of them.* Still, the blue in those eyes did bring to her mind the image of crystal waters at a tropical beach somewhere.

Thinking about those eyes now on the moonlit beach, she held his hand as they walked in the direction of the house. It annoyed her when he tossed the empty beer can on the sand, but she let it go for now. She'd make sure he picked it up on the way back.

Holding her hand, strolling through the sand, it struck Devon that she certainly wasn't the type of girl that his parents would approve of. The fact was they wanted him to go to school back home in the Northeast. If not Ivy League, they could have at least gotten him into Boston College, or even a good small school, like Providence, or Bryant, in Rhode Island. But he was tired of the New England winters, and he had let his parents know it. He wanted to go to school where the weather was warmer, and the college girls stayed more scantily-clad for a longer season. To pacify them, he did manage to keep his grades up. By the time of his senior year, they had to agree that he could have done a lot worse than N.C. State.

She wasn't what he would call a beautiful girl, what with the way she dressed, her dirty-blond hair, and her petite mouth. She was more what he would call cute. However, tonight, after five or six beers, she looked absolutely gorgeous to him in the moonlight. He also reasoned that even a young lady in a burlap-looking skirt can be persuaded to hike that skirt way up above her thighs.

Now, if her panties turn out to be burlap, that would be a little too weird, he thought to himself.

She gripped his hand a little tighter and said, "You know, Cape Cod, you didn't have to make fun of Billy Joe like that."

"Oh come on," he whined, "he's just a good ole' Southern boy. I was just joking with him."

She let go of his hand, stopped walking, and glared at him. "You know, he's not the only one here who's from the South."

He realized that he had offended her; and might blow his chances. "Hey, I didn't mean anything by it, really. I'm sorry if I got you mad. I really do like the guy; it was just the beers talking a little too much." He rubbed her left arm and shoulder gently, and she let him.

The feel of his hand on her shoulder seemed to soften her a bit. "Okay, just remember where you are, and how what you say can affect people, right?"

"I know, I know," he said. After a slight hesitation, he asked, "So, what do you want to do for the rest of the night?" He tried to disguise his leer with a smile.

She grinned at him and glanced briefly down the beach. "I want to go check out the haunted house."

Hesitating, he looked in that direction, and then back at her. "Why? You don't really think it's haunted, do you?"

"If it is, we might be able to communicate with the spirits." That was part of the whole sixties thing with Sookie. There was a spirit world out there, she was sure, and she felt in tune with it. She'd done her share of reading about séances, and believed she could figure out how to

176

moonlight, as her dress straps had fallen down. It wouldn't take much effort now for the rest of it to come off.

She jumped up and banged into him, knocking him back a few steps. She screamed at his contact. "You frightened me! I didn't know you were there!"

"Frightened you? Sookie, come on, there's no ghosts here!"

"No!" she yelled. "Devon, it's blood. It's the dried blood from that woman. Didn't Billy Joe say that her husband murdered her, and there was blood everywhere?" Suddenly, she didn't want to be there anymore. She didn't want to be a medium channeling spirits, a ghost whisperer. "Devon, let's go. I want to get out of here."

"Oh, come on, Sookie. This place has had so much water hit it through the years; it's probably just a huge damp spot."

"No!" she stammered at him, "Devon, please, let's go!"

At that point, the combination of the lust and the beer, and the thought of not getting what he wanted, angered him. "No." He lunged for her, grabbing her head, pulling it to him, and kissed her hard. She tried to pull away, but he moved his hands down to her breasts, and grabbed at them, trying to rip the dress off her.

With her right hand, she reached up and raked his left cheek, drawing blood, pushing away, and yelling, "I said no!" as she did so. Losing her balance from the effort, she fell backwards toward the porch, banging her left arm against where the doors used to be, and cut her wrist on a protruding piece of glass. She yelled out in pain. He let out a yell himself, backing away from her as she fell. Then she staggered to her feet, her hand bloodied.

"Devon, I'm sorry, but . . . Oww! My wrist, oh look at my wrist!"

He didn't care about that. He was too busy feeling blood coming through his fingers that were cupped to his face. "Oh, you son of a . . .! Why? Look what you did to me!" He dropped his hands away from his face and started advancing toward her—nightmarish in the moonlit dark with the blood streaming from his cheek. She shook her head, very afraid of him now.

He ranted "You! You lure me up here like you're some freak who can talk to the dead? You tease me and let me think I'm going to get some? Then you do this to me! What is with that? What is that?"

She shook her head, pleading, "No, Devon, please don't. I'm hurt, look at me!"

But then he stopped short and wasn't looking at her. He was looking past her toward the opening of the porch and the ocean beyond. His eyes were bulging. "What *is* that?"

Coming at them from out of the sea, was a large, reptilian head, scary-white. The room seemed to glow from its approaching luminescence. There was some wet fringe, like feathers, around the long neck which snaked back into the ocean. Just before it reached the broken porch doors, the mouth opened. The teeth were crocodilian, only larger, and there were many of them. A black tongue shot in and out.

Devon screamed and fell backwards on the floor. As the creature cocked its head sideways to attack, Sookie turned just in time to see its jaws snap tight around her torso. Her blood gushed forth as she was lifted off the floor and out over the beach.

182

She managed one scream for help at Devon, before the agony of feeling her pelvis, rib cage, and viscera being fused into one mouthful silenced her for good. Devon gaped in sobering shock—the blood from his cheek spattering onto his shirtfront.

The creature gave one seemingly accusatory look of its crimson eye at Devon before it pulled back, and drew its long white neck and head out into the sea. In the moonlight, he caught a brief glimpse of Sookie's blood-matted hair, and her open, but dead eyes. Her legs, with her skirt hiked up just the way he had wanted it, dangled from the side of the creature's mouth as it went under the water. *She's with the spirits now*, he crazily thought to himself.

He winced from the damage to his cheek. The pain seemed to bring him to his senses, and he scrambled to his feet, whimpering. He made it halfway down the stairs before jumping off, landing hands and knees first onto the sand surrounding the haunted house of Avon. There was fresh pain in his right palm, making him cry out. He had landed on some sharp debris when he fell on the floor, and now had a fresh cut. He got to his feet, cursing in pain and fright, and looked out past the house toward the sea. The moon was still bright on the crashing waves, and the water gleamed white.

As fast as he could, Devon ran from the house through the deep sand, whimpering in pain as he ran. His blood trickled off from him, dropping onto the beach.

Up the beach, he could make out two dark figures lying by the dying bonfire. It was Bryan and Mandy. They had both passed out, failing to consummate their lust that night.

183

Devon screamed for help as he staggered toward them. Here the beach was sloped and difficult to run on. There was no response from those two, but further up from them, he could see two other figures running in his direction.

Joe and Tara had decided to walk north along the beach before they went home. Because of the direction of the wind, they couldn't be sure, but thought they had heard screams and turned toward the sound. They had started to walk toward Bryan and Mandy to ask if they'd heard anything. That was when they saw the dark figure stumbling up the beach. They realized it was Devon and started running toward him, wondering where Sookie was.

Devon saw them now. "Help, guys, help!" He staggered a few more steps and then fell forward into the sand. He stared at the granules. They shone too much, even in this bright moonlight. Turning and glancing up toward where the moon should have been, he saw the whitish glow, but it wasn't the moon.

Up the beach, Joe and Tara were running as fast as they could toward Devon. He was still beyond where the other couple had passed out, but they could see him clearly down on his knees in the sand. Suddenly, they both stopped. "Hey!" Joe yelled, and was pointing. Tara followed his arm. "Do you see that wave?" he asked, "look at the curl over the beach!"

Tara marveled at it. "Why is it so . . . white?"

They both heard it for a second. It was a horrified scream as the glowing overtook Devon, and then the scream stopped.

It was no wave. It was as if the moon had come down and opened like an impossibly huge mouth as it snatched Devon up. Joe and Tara looked on in shock as they saw it recede back toward the water. That glow. It looked just like a ghost. The only other color was the demon-red eye, and the dark outline of Devon McCabe's legs dangling from its mouth as it disappeared beneath the sea.

They tried to tell the police as best they could what they'd seen. The authorities were skeptical, of course. They found Bryan and Mandy still passed out on the beach, snoring through the whole thing. Obviously, all of them had been drinking. How could they know what they'd seen?

The police found fresh blood at the house, but there was no evidence to link the others to any foul play. It was concluded that something had gone violently wrong between Devon and Sookie. Bodies were never recovered. The authorities surmised that the sea had claimed them.

But Sookie's and Devon's parents weren't satisfied. They suspected the other four knew more than they were saying, and didn't believe a word of the wild story about some monster coming out of the sea. They had a lot of money to hire their own investigators and made life miserable for the other parents, not shying away from making their suspicions public.

The sensational news of the disappearance, and the pressure from the grieving parents, affected the other four college students. Their grades suffered and, eventually, they dropped out of N.C. State. Once out of school, they drifted away from each other, and lost contact with anyone from their college days. Their future didn't hold much promise. Because of this, many of the locals say that, in a sense, the Sea Ghost of Avon had not just gotten Sookie and Devon, but those other four college kids as well.

Despite the best efforts of the local authorities to have the house torn down, amazingly, the Outer Banks Historical Society managed to save it. However ill-gotten its reputation, the house had an even bigger history behind it now. Curious tourists would want to see it, just like they flock to see that other house further up north in Rodanthe that they made a movie about.

Out in the depths, the creature moved through the abyss, its Cyclops crimson eye guiding it, and a glowing trail briefly lingering behind in the murk. It was an animal. It knew nothing about ghosts, or why the prey above the waves believed in ghosts. The desires of this prey, and why they caused each other such pain, were beyond the comprehension of its primitive brain. Mere hunger—with a desire to hunt, not to haunt, drove it forward.

Propelled by that hunger and instinct, it knew it would again return sometime to that place, if not now, maybe 10 years from now, although it had no concept of time. It would just know when to return for a filling meal.

It moved on. The oceans are vast, with many places to hunt. Wherever it swam, above the waves it could smell blood and follow the scent. Despite the creature not knowing why, it had learned that this prey could always be counted on to cut each other.

For this one, I have to thank my brother-in-law and his family for sharing their home with us on visits to Tucson, Arizona. With them living on the edge of the desert and being able to look out on that amazing landscape, I was inspired to write this one. So, thank you Jim, Denise, and young Sophia. Sophia! Get away from your cell phone for a few moments and read this cool little story that Uncle Dan wrote!

DRINKING IN THE DESERT: A STORY OF THE SAGUARO

The Saguaros were looking very stately this evening. Or, were they looking very imposing? Cotton Dalrymple wasn't sure. He squinted at the dusk settling into the Tucson desert. Crow's feet bordered his weather-beaten eyes—their color looked like dulled blue paint. He was just finishing his second glass of mezcal, a good enough brand from the Oaxaca region of Mexico. He hadn't shaved in several days, and the aroma of the liquor seemed to hang on his gray whiskers like drops of dew. The buzz in his head was starting to swirl like a desert breeze in autumn, and his discernment of different objects out there had become partly cloudy.

At $65 a bottle, it wasn't something that he would buy himself. It had been a gift from an ex-buddy whom he had served with on the force. Out of spite against that buddy, he hadn't wanted to drink the stuff, so it had sat in one of his kitchen cabinets for about a year. But he had relented and dug it out a couple of weeks ago when his other liquor bottles started running dry. He finished the rest of the glass and tried not to wince as he felt the pleasurable burn slip down his throat. Silently, he mused to himself that a tough cop, even a tough ex-cop, should be able to handle hard liquor like it was water.

He had been told by the ex-buddy that, "Not all mezcals are tequila, but all tequilas are mezcal. Some of the high-end brands of this stuff can go for five hundred bucks a bottle." He'd further explained that the difference between this and tequila had something to do with the type of agave plant that was used in the fermentation. Cotton couldn't remember exactly which agave it was, but he didn't care. All that mattered at this moment was that he had developed a fonder taste for this stuff, rather than tequila.

He chuckled to himself, thinking that he could always try to call his ex-buddy tonight to ask him what the exact difference was. Of course, that wasn't going to happen, seeing as neither his ex-buddy, nor his old partner, nor any of the other cops on the City of Tucson Police Department, would probably ever want to talk to him again, not after the incident on the job and his subsequent "early retirement."

Oh well, he thought, *maybe it isn't the $500 high-end brand, but I'll still manage to tolerate the $65 a-bottle stuff somehow.* After all, it wasn't his money that had been spent on it.

Looking back again at the Saguaros, he was fascinated at how much they stood out. Of course, they always dominated the scenery among the other cacti: the painful huascha, with their fat spear-like and serrated-edged leaves, the tempting prickly pear, and the flowering barrel variety. There were also Palo Verde, ironwood, and mesquite trees that peppered the landscape behind his modular home. But the Saguaros were the titans of this desert; and this evening, for some reason, the giant cacti had an even starker appearance than usual.

Cotton had long been impressed by these silent giants, some of them centuries old, standing up to the elements of this climate; changes in temperature (the desert can get cold at night), sandstorms and, of course, flash floods produced by the rains after periods of drought.

The wind was picking up. Tonight it seemed that a thunderstorm was imminent, which might result in one of those flash floods through the wash just beyond his property line. Flashes of heat lightning could be seen over the city, east of Cotton's home. The Rincon Mountains beyond, and the more prominent Catalinas to the north, reflected the bursts of electric light from the heavens.

He sometimes let his imagination pace about, especially after a few drinks, and wondered what the Saguaros were doing out there. Were they pointing to some mystery in the sky—a secret that they would never reveal? Or, were they just giant middle fingers flipping us all off? Yes, they could be whimsical to look at, too. There were two, in particular, out there behind his home, about 50 feet apart, that looked like they were eager to meet. There was the "male" with a shorter stalk, strategically growing in place, curving up and erect. It faced the "female," which had two larger stalks extending out to its sides. It was the image in Cotton's head of a woman with her legs spread and slightly bent at the knees, waiting to receive her man. Such were the things that Cotton thought about after not being with a woman for over a year, and then hitting heavy on the mezcal to try and dull the ache.

But, all whimsy aside, perhaps it was something else about the Saguaros? People can't live for a longtime around places like Tucson and the other cities and towns in the four corner western states, Arizona, New Mexico, Colorado, and Utah, and not hear the stories and legends of the Native American tribes that once roamed those lands in great numbers. Cotton was no exception. He knew of a tale from the Pima Indians that revealed how the Saguaro came to be. It had to do with two children, a brother and sister,

190

who ran away from their mother after she spanked them for playing too rough, and then knocking over the porridge that she was cooking. They ran away to the hills, which were quite bare. Upon seeing that there was no vegetation, the little girl said, "Let us become beautiful plants to fill these hills," and she turned into the lovely, green Palo Verde tree. However, her brother, being more rambunctious, and possessed by the warrior spirit, turned into the Saguaro instead. He told his sister, "I will produce fruit, and live forever." When their mother came to find them, she tried to embrace her son, but the spines on his giant stalk stabbed at her—killing her. It was punishment for her being so cruel in spanking them when they had meant no harm in knocking over the porridge. Thus, were both the Palo Verde and the Saguaro born.

The Saguaros were silent witnesses to that warrior spirit coming to life many times through numerous years, and the invasion of the white man was only one of the many wars that had been fought. In this area, there was plenty of history of Navajo and Apache tribes fighting against each other, raiding the other's territory for goods, livestock, and young women. The land had known much bloodshed. In fact, the ground where Cotton's home now stood had once been Apache territory.

But if the Saguaros are the noble witnesses and the titans of the desert, then the javelinas are the lowly swine. In the remaining dim light of evening, highlighted by flashes of lightning, sitting on his wicker chair on his back porch, Cotton could see a whole group of them starting to gather just this side of the wash. No . . . wait. It wasn't just a group. They seemed to be swarming. It was more like a horde, multiplying in number as he watched. With the mezcal doing a lazy river float inside his head, he extracted his tired, six-foot-two frame from the wicker chair.

Cotton believed they were named after a javelin because some people, including him, would like nothing more than to lift them up and throw them an Olympic distance. Actually, the name comes from the sharp tusks they have, which reminded the Spaniards of spears. They've been referred to as rodents, but are really a type of peccary—too big to be a rat, but too small to be a wild boar, even though they can be as nasty as one. Despite that, there are people, other than Cotton, who think they are just so adorable. Maybe they're not so adorable after they get into your trash cans and make a mess by strewing garbage all over your property.

But these tonight didn't look like they were on the hunt for refuse. The horde of them was looking in Cotton's direction. It was the eyes that he noticed most—they looked unnatural. They were like embers burning in the piggish faces. He would catch a glint of that hideous eye light every moment or so reflecting off their jutting tusks. There was a sizzling sound that Cotton at first thought was emanating from around their cloven hooves. Then he realized it was coming from the drool hitting the sand as it slithered off those tusks.

They were grunting and squealing at each other, in between turning their faces away, and then looking straight back at him, with what looked to Cotton like sheer contempt. It was almost as if . . .well, as if they were *communicating*, coming up with some kind of strategy.

The lightning flashes became more frequent now— no rain, just the electricity in the air. The flashes snapped like bullwhips across the sky, and they had an eerie, reddish color. It was during one of these flashes that Cotton noticed that it wasn't just the javelinas gathering. There was something else grouping around the javelinas. Now the ground was churning, and there were loud clicks, and other sounds like bones grinding against each other. Amid the frequent flashes, Cotton recognized them. They were scorpions, but too large to be in these parts—too large to be in any parts. There was something about the stingers that was abnormal, too. It wasn't poison. It was fire—small bursts of fire shooting out from them, like little flamethrowers scorching the ground.

But there weren't just scorpions. There were also spiders—big spiders. These weren't desert tarantulas; they were too large for that. These were the size of kittens, crawling all over the larger scorpions, and the legs of the javelinas. Neither the scorpions, nor the javelinas, seemed to mind. It was as if the spiders were positioning themselves strategically on their allies to unleash a multi-pronged attack. In the flashes, Cotton could make out their eyes—too many eyes. Something black and syrupy oozed from the spiders where their fangs would be, and also made a sizzling sound as it hit the dirt.

Lastly was the writhing. They were snakes, coiling and undulating all over themselves in advance of the hordes behind them. The heads were all pointed in Cotton's direction. The rattles shook and made an unearthly chiming sound, like haunted bells. This wasn't a warning that you were getting too close, as a rattler would normally do. This was more of a clarion call, as if sounding a charge into battle.

It was as if all the frightening denizens of the desert had joined together to make war. War against whom, Cotton? Or was this to be some greater battle than just the consumption of one man? Cotton was standing upright, alert now, blinking his eyes between the flashes of lightning, taking it all in. His heart was beating hard, and he felt cold fear, worse than the fear that he had felt having to venture down some dark alleys when he was on the job.

His glass was empty. He took the bottle of mezcal and poured himself another stiff one, about two thumbs full. Downing it in one quick shot, he squeezed his eyes shut. *He had to be seeing things.* He opened his eyes, hoping they would all be gone. They weren't standing there anymore. Instead, they were advancing toward his modular home, toward him. He dropped the glass, letting it shatter on the concrete porch, and ran inside his back door.

Cotton felt that he had no choice now but to call his ex-buddy from the force, regardless of whether the guy would want to speak to him. Inside, he pulled his flip phone out of his pocket—his only choice of communication, since he could not afford a more expensive cellular plan—another consequence of his forced retirement. His heart pounding, he shakily pushed the numbers, which he still knew by rote. The phone rang several times while Cotton nervously watched the activity increasing outside his back windows. It was as if some huge, roiling black wave was breaking over itself as the legion advanced toward the back of his house.

Finally, Valdez picked up. There was silence on the other end. Cotton tried his best to be calm and cordial, and asked, "Valdez! Que pasa, amigo? How's it going?"

"What do you want, Cotton?" The annoyance in Valdez's voice was evident. Cotton was surprised that he had even answered the phone.

"Hey, is that any way to talk to an old buddy? What about a little love for old time's sake, huh?"

"You're lucky I even picked up, *cabron*. So, again I ask, what do you want?"

Still holding a grudge, insulting me like that, Cotton thought. "Look, there's some really strange stuff going on in the desert behind my house. I need a cop to come out and take a look at what's going on here." Cotton looked back out through his windows again. He didn't need the flashes of lighting anymore to see that the swarm was now getting closer to his home. "And, I need someone fast!"

"What kind of strange stuff?" Valdez asked. Cotton knew that, as much as Valdez might dislike him, he was still a cop and had to register a call from a civilian.

"Well," Cotton continued, "it's kind of hard to explain."

"Try me."

"Well . . . it's really hard to explain. It has to do with some strange behavior with the animals out there, the javelinas, they're like giant rats, and there are even the scorpions. And, and . . ."

"And what, Cotton?"

Temporarily distracted, he mumbled back into the phone. "Snakes . . . and spiders—you really have to see it yourself to understand what's going on."

From the tone of his voice, Cotton could picture Valdez letting out an exasperated sigh. "Cotton, are you finally hitting that mezcal that I bought you? I'd be surprised if you even had any left."

195

"Look Valdez, it ain't the mezcal, and yes, I've had a couple...okay maybe a few, but this ain't the liquor talking. I'm telling you there's something really strange, and scary going on out here, and I need help ASAP!"

It was obvious that Valdez had no patience left. "Look, cabron, it's apparent that you've been drinking, and I don't know what your true motive is for calling, but you've got a hell of a lot of nerve calling here—especially after you disgraced yourself and had to leave the job—with this stupid story about strange desert animals behind your house. I suggest you just give it up, go to bed, and sleep it off."

Cotton's nerves were stretched thin, and he snapped, "What do you mean after I 'disgraced myself'? I was just doing my job, and I got forced out because of it. You know that!"

Now it was Valdez's turn to snap. "Doing your job? That's a riot! You busted a 16-year old Chicano kid, just for smoking weed, of all things! Then you scare the kid into trying to be an informant to get at some meth dealers, by telling him that his mother is going to be deported if he doesn't cooperate. You, asshole! You got that kid killed!"

Cotton looked away from the frightening activity outside the window for a moment, staring silently at the floor with the phone to his ear. He couldn't deny what Valdez had said.

"Yeah, I thought so," Valdez said. "Don't call here again, ever."

Cotton responded, "Okay, well, I ain't got time for this right now, and you don't have to worry about me ever calling back again."

Despite the more pressing, ominous circumstances developing in his back yard, Cotton just had to get in one more dig at Valdez. "Listen, I hope one day you figure out a better way to get the job done when the Chief is riding your ass to make more arrests and to get the dealers off the streets and deported, no matter how you get it done. Hey, have a nice career, *ese!*"

"Oh, I swear! I can't believe you said that! No creo! Don't you call me that, Cotton, don't you ever call me that ag . . ."

But he didn't hear the rest, as he snapped the phone shut. Breathing deeply, he looked out the window again, seeing the unnatural hordes creeping closer to his domicile. He was going to have to try and handle this himself. Fueled as much now by anger and alcohol—as well as fear—he went for his guns.

Since he hadn't actually been fired from the force, Cotton had no problem still purchasing guns. In his bedroom, he grabbed his weapons from the closet, frantically loaded them with ammo, and tossed each one on his unmade bed, as he finished loading.

First, he grabbed the handgun. When he was on the job, Cotton had carried a standard-issue 9mm Glock. However, by giving him the name "Cotton," his parents must have thought there was a latent cowboy hiding inside him somewhere, which would probably explain why he just had to have a revolver. He smiled briefly and shook his head slightly at the thought, as he tossed his .357 Magnum onto the bed. He had bought the snub-nosed version because it was better for "conceal and carry" purposes. He now regretted that because of the task at hand—as a long barrel would be more accurate. Too late, his snub-nosed model would have to do.

Next, he brought out his hunting rifle. For this, Cotton had settled on a Timber Classic Marlin. It was a "lever" gun, as opposed to a bolt-action rifle—again, a cowboy thing. A regular Lucas McCain, he was. Besides its portability and easy handling, it had a better magazine capacity than many bolt action rifles and, at about $600, he could afford it on his reduced pension.

Last to come out of the closet was his shotgun. Here, the cowboy influence ended. It was a Mossburg 500 Combo, a pump action, two-barrel, 12 gauge. At about $500, it was a real bargain. This gun was supposed to be used for hunting turkey and deer. Cotton hoped it would work on unearthly peccaries, arthropods, and slithering reptiles instead.

He stuffed the .357 into the waistband of his jeans and held the two rifles between his arm and side. Grabbing an extra set of shells for the Mossburg, he headed out the back door again. Once on the porch, he gasped and swore. They were almost upon him, seeming like thousands upon thousands. *Where in the hell were they all coming from? How did this happen?*

Suddenly, the lightning began striking the desert in a succession of bolts—like red lasers. Cotton was knocked back into his wicker chair—his weapons falling to the ground around him. He watched in shock and fright as the mighty bolts struck Saguaro after Saguaro. The ground began to rumble, as if from an earthquake.

Cotton cried out, "Oh no! Oh, my dear God, no! This is it! This is the end, the end of it all, happening right here!" The unholy swarm was at the edge of the concrete, ready to engulf him. It was a roiling, slithering, grunting and squealing mass of tusks, and fangs, clanging rattles, and stinging fire. And then there were the eyes. There was so much evil red in those eyes. They bore into him with their accusatory sight, condemning him. He felt guilt closing in, as if some massive object was pressing him down into the earth, suffocating him for his sins.

No time for penance now, standing quickly, he grabbed the Magnum to fire into the crushing, poisonous horde. At that moment, there was a tremendous, blinding flash, and a booming noise like nothing Cotton had ever heard before, as a bolt hit the Saguaro closest to his home. He was knocked down to the ground—the Magnum clattering uselessly away from him, amongst his fallen rifles. Before the horde was upon him, he managed to scramble to his feet and rush in his back door. He collapsed, unconscious, onto his kitchen floor.

Light. There was light outside the film of his eyelids. His head pounded with pain. It was as if there was some evil imp inside his skull, banging away with a hammer. Cotton opened his crusty eyes and found he was staring at the motionless ceiling fan in his kitchen. From his position, laid out on the dirty floor, he realized that it was sunlight hastening in through the blinds on his kitchen windows.

It was morning. *What in the hell happened last night?* He managed to sit up and lean back against the sink cabinet. Looking up at the wall above him, the clock ticked to 10 minutes before seven. The ticking clock worked in unison with the imp in his head—a rhythmic pounding. He rubbed his temples and closed his eyes.

Standing up, he splashed some cold water onto his face. He looked up at the blinds but couldn't see outside because of the glare coming through. Gradually, he remembered the events of the night. But he was still here. *It never happened at all*, he thought. It was that damned mezcal. As he had done on more than one occasion before, he swore to himself to never touch the stuff again.

He walked out the back door into the sunlight. The broken drinking glass reflected it. Besides the broken glass, the first things he noticed were his guns lying about the concrete patio. He swore at himself, shaking his head. "Stupid, stupid, stupid! You stupid, dumb ass! You left your weapons lying around outside last night in the storm, because you were drunk! Oh, how could I be so stupid?" But as he leaned over to pick up the shotgun, the odor suddenly hit him, and he stood up, squinting into the sunlight—with his hand trying to shield his eyes.

The carnage was massive. There were dead carcasses of javelina everywhere—hundreds, no, maybe thousands, in massive heaps, both on his property, and beyond the wash. There was a coating on many of them—some ugly, black ochre. Cotton assumed that was the spiders, their bodies rotted, and boiled up as part of the stinking masses. Useless scorpion stingers could be seen sticking up out of the black ooze that coated the dead javelinas, and there were motionless rattles also visible, like broken toy bells, no longer ringing of doom and destruction. Where he could see eyes on the javelinas, they were all lifeless. No evil red glow shone out from them.

Cotton began to walk among them. He had a handkerchief in his pocket and held that up against his nose and mouth because of the stench. Flies were buzzing everywhere. Then he noticed something most fantastic. There were masses of spines—needles—that were sticking into the javelina. They'd been impaled by them, so numerous that Cotton thought that the creatures looked like grotesque pin cushions.

He recognized these needles. They were from the Saguaros. He had forgotten about them. Now he remembered how the lightning bolts had hit them. Looking around in astonishment, he saw that not a single Saguaro had been felled. They weren't even charred. Straining his eyes to see more into the distance, he saw some Saguaros, standing still straight and tall, with javelinas impaled upon them, the entrails of the nasty peccaries plopping to the ground below the giant cacti. It was a smorgasbord for the flies.

Cotton thought to himself, *this wasn't the mezcal. How did these javelinas get impaled on the Saguaros? Something happened out here last night, something that is unreal, yet it's all too real. Look around yourself, Cotton.* It was a post-apocalyptic, desert graveyard. The javelinas, and their creeping, slithering allies, all dead, and he hadn't fired a single shot. He looked at the carcasses with the needles impaled through them, and then again looked around at the Saguaros. He stared at one of the Saguaros and asked, "How can this be? Giant cactus, what are you, after all?"

Cotton wondered what Valdez and the other cops would think of this. The massive stink would reach the city, and they would be forced to come out and investigate. Would Valdez still think it was just the mezcal talking? Cotton knew just what he would ask him: *What's happened here, ese? Can you explain it? Lo que paso aqui? Por favor, explique, por favor.*

He gingerly made his way back to his house through the fetid masses. It was as if the word had spread among the buzzing insects, and every fly and its third cousin were now descending upon the feast. As he returned to his porch, the sound was incessant, but rhythmic somehow. Carried by the soft morning breezes, the thrumming sounded to Cotton like a drum beat. There was something else in that sound—like a faint chanting, a soft whooping noise, like a war cry, or rather, a song of victory. It reminded him of the ceremonial singing he had once heard at a Native American festival.

Looking at the giant cactus closest to his home, he thought again of the legend of that Pima Indian boy becoming the Saguaro—that boy—the one with the warrior spirit growing within. Many people thought that the Navajo Wind Talkers, so prominently portrayed in the movies and other media, who fought in World War II, were the exception. But Cotton knew that was untrue. He knew that it is a tradition, and a duty, among many Native American tribes to defend the homeland. Despite centuries of oppression, displacement, and slaughter, they would still defend it, even if it had been subjugated by the white man.

Cotton gazed at his close Saguaro. Slowly, he raised his hand as a gesture of thanks and gave it a knowing nod of his head. He had been spared this apocalypse, or at least mini-apocalypse, by the giant cacti, and he didn't know why. But he would find out. This was a calling. He now knew that—despite his past—there was a purpose for him still being there, a purpose greater than just drinking the rest of his life away in the desert. The Saguaros remained there tall and motionless, in silent acceptance of his grateful acknowledgment. In time, perhaps the warrior spirit would speak to him somehow, and reveal what he was to do next. He would be patient and listen for it.

Now he heard sirens. He looked up and saw in the distance a caravan of cars, lights flashing and sirens screaming, as they raced along Calle del Patria, to eventually reach his home. The cloud of dust they stirred from the dirt road rose up and embraced the fouled air. Cotton picked up his guns, brought them back into the house, and secured them in his bedroom. Then he went out front to wait and greet his old brethren from the Tucson PD.

I was trying to come up with one more story for this collection, and this is it, so it naturally appears last in the book. I went by myself to a local movie house near our home one weekday morning to catch a bargain matinee showing of a movie called "Hereditary." I was the only person in the theatre. It was a film that was creepy, scary, and disturbing, all rolled into one—probably not a good one to watch by yourself. Although absorbed in the movie, I was still aware of my surroundings: dim lights, the shifting of shadows in corners and under the seats, and the fact that I was alone. In such a setting, the imagination has a tendency to take off, and the idea for this story was born. My apologies regarding the word play in the title to any yoga enthusiasts out there. It may work for you, but it's just not for me.

LE CINAMASTE FANTASTIQUE

The movie originally debuted at the Cannes Film Festival. Some of the English-speaking film critics, trying to impress their French counterparts, described it as "c'est magnifique," and "une joie pour les sens," or, a "joy to the senses." Whatever language was used to critique it, *Namaste to the Gods*, was a hit, and not to be missed. In his review, the movie critic in Ralph Wagner's local paper, the *Sarasota Herald Tribune*, had added the instruction, "Do not see this movie alone." Ralph assumed this was because the sensory experience of it all should be shared with a friend or significant other.

Well, Ralph *was* going to see it alone. His significant other, Doris, had left him a year ago, which was two years after they had moved to Florida. Thirty-two years of marriage were whisked away by a ball point pen when he scribbled his signature on divorce papers. There had been no children. Biologically, that was his fault, not hers. Adoption was not on the table either, as he was opposed to it. If she had hinted to him now and then through the years that she was upset about their childless marriage, he had never taken the hint. The accumulated benefits from his lab job with the pharmaceutical company, and her career that concluded with a pension from a county in Maryland, together with never having to spend money on raising children, had provided a comfortable retirement portfolio for both of them in the Sunshine State. In making the move down South, Doris considered the money they had accumulated from never having to raise children as a bittersweet consolation.

205

Once they moved to Florida, Doris frequently repeated her other desires for them to travel, to take up new hobbies; something to fill the gap of having no children to visit them, nor grandchildren to spoil.   But Ralph's obsession with seeing movies had continued. He spent too much time inside of theatres to take advantage of the climate and other pursuits. His grayish-white skin, the color of sheetrock, confirmed this.

Occasionally, he would speak to her about his thoughts of actually pursuing some type of acting career in retirement. There are, after all, extras needed on the sets of TV shows and films. He could see about getting a start that way, as an extra, maybe catch the eye of an agent, and then who knows where that might lead to? This Doris actually encouraged, at least it would inject some thrill into their lives. But in time she came to realize that it was all just dreamy talk. It became apparent to her that Ralph was more interested in just going to the movies, instead of trying to be in them.

Some people obsess over food, or drink and other substances, or over computer and video games. However, throughout their whole marriage, and despite working for a drug company, Ralph's narcotic of choice had always been the film. It even weighed upon their decision to ever have children. On the question of adoption, Ralph had once said to her that, "Adopting a child would be like stealing a movie that you hadn't paid for, it's like video piracy."

In disbelief, she summarized to him, "In other words, you're saying we can't take someone else's child when we haven't paid the price for having our own."

"Exactly!" he cheerily responded. After that exchange, she never brought up the question of having children again.

Once she was resigned to the fact that the obsession was going to last into their retirement here in Florida, Doris was finished. Ralph was blinded by Hollywood's big lights, and never saw the divorce coming until it was too late. Before they had even finished paying off their attorneys, he found out that she was already seeing someone else. He ran into them together once at the Winn-Dixie Supermarket. Doris introduced her new man to Ralph, no awkwardness at all on her part. The guy's name was Dmitri, or something like that. Ralph took some delight in noticing that Dmitri had a larger paunch around the middle than he did, but Doris didn't seem to mind. Dmitri liked to travel, and he had a tan.

When it was all over, Ralph wondered about it for a while, trying to figure out what had gone wrong. Then he started going back to the morning matinees again to console himself. Maybe it was better this way. Doris finally got what she had wanted in moving to Florida, and he still had what he had always loved.

He liked to attend the Old Time Sarasota Cinema. It was a small, family-owned theatre located in a strip mall, not 10 minutes from the home that he and Doris once shared. It was 20 minutes for him now, driving from the apartment he was living in. Doris had gotten the home in the divorce settlement. That was fine with Ralph. His large screen TV still fit on the wall in his new, smaller place.

The owners had spent just enough on the theatre and its lobby to keep it clean and efficient, so it didn't exactly look "old time" anymore. Still, Ralph saw it as a more intimate setting than the megaplex chains that seem to be in every shopping mall—with their reclining chairs, booming sound systems, and such. Some of them even served overpriced, watered-down alcoholic drinks now, to be accompanied by fancy tapas dining selections. *Tapas in a theatre? How ridiculous.* It was just like the ballparks offering all kinds of fancy selections these days. Whatever happened to a good old hot dog and a beer? Between megaplexes and gourmet sushi at ballparks, it was just too much extravagance for Ralph.

Best of all about this theater was the lower price of the tickets. Every movie, every day, shown before 12 noon was six bucks. Sometimes they got new releases right away, sometimes not. Ralph didn't mind. He had all the time in the world to wait for the latest release to come to his theatre, now that Doris was gone, busy with her new life seeing the sights with Dmitri.

Namaste to the Gods was one of those movies that had been out for a while and finally made it to the Old Time Sarasota Cinema. None of the morning matinee movies were ever crowded at this place, especially on a weekday such as this Tuesday, so there was never a shortage of seats. He purchased his ticket at the outside window and went in to the concession stand. In his right pocket, he had a miniature replica of a golden statue. He had purchased it, treating it as a souvenir, at a novelty store that sold knock-off Hollywood memorabilia. On his way into the theatre, he absent-mindedly caressed it in his pocket.

As with the price of tickets, the cost of food at this theatre was lower, relative to the megaplexes. He purchased a bottle of water, and a medium-sized popcorn, and then went to the dispenser to put on that stuff that masquerades as butter, and—just like the synthetic oil that now goes into automobiles—has a viscosity that's good for about 7000 miles. Ralph loaded it on and filled an extra condiment container of the goo to add for when he got halfway through his bucket.

He proceeded to the usher taking the tickets—no other patrons around him at the moment. The usher had an intellectual disability. In Ralph's earlier days, such a person was referred to as mentally retarded, or mentally challenged. Ralph tried to push that expression out of his mind as he approached the young man. "Jeffrey" was in a motorized wheelchair in the center of the corridor. He raised thick fingers and, smiling through thick lips, and with slightly out of focus eyes gazing at Ralph asked, "Ticket, please?" Ralph handed him his ticket, hoping that the young man would not try to engage him in any conversation.

Handing Ralph back his half of the ticket, he simply said, "Theatre four, just slightly to your left. Enjoy the movie, sir."

"Thank you."

As Ralph began to walk past, Jeffrey turned his head and asked, "Sir, are you going to this movie alone?"

Ralph stopped and asked, "Why yes, is that some kind of problem?"

Jeffrey hesitated a moment. Despite his intellectual disability, Ralph thought that his face suddenly looked very lucid and serious. "Just be careful, sir," Jeffrey said.

"Careful—about what?"

Again, Jeffrey hesitated. "Just be careful; watch your step, sir. There's light, but it's still very dark in there, especially when no one else is around."

Ralph slowly nodded, as if thanking him for the common sense warning, and turned again, continuing on to theatre number four. He didn't see that Jeffrey's eyes, though slightly out of focus, had a concerned look to them, a somewhat sad look, and that he was no longer smiling through his thick lips.

Upon entering the theatre, it seemed illuminated enough to Ralph. There were the lines of small guide dot lights along either wall and on the lighted exit signs. But mostly the illumination came from the advertisements that were being shown on the screen. Ralph was used to that by now. Despite paying for admission to the movie, one was also subjected these days to feature-sized, blaring commercials advertising everything from soda to smart phones to car sales. Then there would be the MPAA-approved previews of upcoming new releases. With these seemingly endless previews, Ralph knew that if a movie was advertised to start at 10:30, it would be about 10:45 before the feature actually began. This way, he could gauge when it would actually let out, in case he had something important to get to in the afternoon. However, it was a rare afternoon that Ralph had anything important to get to these days, what with Doris out and about with her new man, Dmitri—that pudgy guy with his Russian accent and tan.

The remarkable thing he noticed this morning was that he was absolutely the only person in the theatre. This he had never experienced before. Would he actually have a private screening? Even on a Tuesday morning, at this low price, surely, with the popularity of this movie, someone else would be attending? *Oh well*, he thought, *now I really have my selection of seats. Better get to the best before anyone else comes in.* He chose an aisle and seat that were basically in the middle of the upper tier.

He half-watched the coming attractions, keeping an eye out for any other patrons who might enter. His fingers fiddled with the popcorn he put to his mouth, as he kept looking over at the entrance. The words of the reviewer in the *Herald Tribune* occasionally came to mind: *Do not see this movie alone.*

"But why should I care if anyone else is in here watching it with me?" he asked the large screen and the empty seats. He shook his head. The previews were done, and the movie was getting ready to start. Ralph shoved in another oily handful of popcorn as the courtesy announcement about not using cell phones kicked in. He had turned his phone off well before entering the theatre. The screen and theatre got darker, and he stopped looking to see if anyone else was coming in to watch the movie with him.

It opened with a definition, large white letters on an all-black screen, "*Namaste: the divine in me bows to the divine in you.*"

Ralph loved the movie; it was mesmerizing. The lead actor was someone previously unknown to him. He was a Siddhartha-like character, someone seemingly on a journey of spiritual discovery to find the meaning of life and wanting to unite the Self with the one true Divine. But the character's visions, portrayed with dazzling effects that permeated Ralph's senses, were the real stars of the show. The character's name was Karjan and, even though his ethnicity was Eastern, it was obvious at the beginning of the movie that he'd been heavily influenced by Western culture.

In his visions, it was as if Karjan was taking a surrealistic magic carpet ride through the world's religions, seeing images of worship and meditation, and gods, and written creeds becoming animated, taking on human shape with mouths spewing forth dogma. Moving alongside him on the ride were colors—various shades of reds, yellows, greens, blues, and purples, undulating above and below each other, like ever-expanding playful tails of kites that fornicated with the wild wind.

There were plants, trees, and animals, morphing briefly into famous human figures from history who would then burst into lotus flower petals, and be swept along with the frenetic colors.

Through all of this, Ralph sat transfixed. He began to imagine himself as playing the part of Karjan—as being Karjan, full of wonder, and yearning, straining to find the Divine, to find that which he should worship. It was as if he was in the mind of Karjan, seeing what was on the screen, but not through his own eyes. He saw through the eyes of the character.

Various gods began to appear. First, he saw a giant, angelic being, with a flaming sword, guarding the entrance to a magnificent garden. The eyes were that of a sentinel, yet there was sorrow in them, as the guardian watched Ralph drift past.

Other gods and goddesses materialized on the journey: There was Kami, of Shinto, the high and auspicious; the "Way" of Taoism, and Ralph trying to hobnob with its Three Purities, the Celestial Worthies; and a trio of the Hindu gods, Brahma, the Creator, Vishnu, the

212

Preserver, and Shiva, the Destroyer, with her many arms and swords. These were followed by the whole Greek pantheon of gods, and then the Roman archaic triad, Jupiter, Mars, and Quirinius. Onward, the parade of deities continued, including those from lesser known religions.

Do not see this movie alone. Why does that sentence keep coming back in my head?

He was vaguely aware of something else happening in the theatre. There was a scraping, wrenching sound that was muffled by the sound coming from the movie. His eyes were still staring at the screen, but out of their corners he saw movement. In the lower tier of the theatre, from right to left, row by row, the seats were coming loose, as if someone was pulling out the bolts from the ground. They began to float, ghostly in the air, and settle down in front of the exits, piling on top of each other, blocking any point of escape. Each row was successively uprooted, and the progress was working its way toward Ralph. He should have been alarmed as the seats in his row and around him began snapping up and floating to the blockades. Instead, he felt a sense of security, and serenity, as if everything was going to be alright. He almost felt the Divine.

Do not see this movie alone.

Do not see this movie alone. He finally knew why. He said to himself aloud, *"Do not see this movie alone, because whoever is there with you can pull you back from the brink."* But he felt okay with this predicament. It was serene, a visual narcotic, all his pain was going away.

There was no going back for Ralph now. There would be no more sequels, no more prequels. He had found his destiny, and he was being drawn to it. Actually, he was floating toward it, drifting past the seats that had uprooted

213

themselves and still stood stacked against the doorways, blocking the exits. Still, there was that feeling of security and serenity. His deity was waiting—that which was worthy of his worship. Ralph took comfort in this.

The drama mask carvings, comedy and tragedy, decorating the walls of the theatre, twisted and gaped in the muted darkness, alternating between grimaces and grins, and always with slit eyes. The strings of guide lights along the floors resembled serpents, as he watched them writhe around the image of a bountiful tree filled with tempting fruit. Ralph was imbued with the wonder, the magic of the movies.

He thought of Doris, and of Dmitri, with his tan and paunch, and his Russian accent. Goodbye to you both, now I've moved on, too. *Ah, Doris, see? I did actually make it into the movies.*

Then he was there, beyond the screen, into the golden land of filmdom. Somewhere in the drifting, he had become naked with nothing from the earth to cover his exposed self, his clothes disintegrating, becoming as the colors floating with the wind behind him. Overcome with emotion, he saw it, what he had always desired. It was the giant, golden god, statue-like, looming many stories high, over him and others who had come before him, as they bowed in naked worship before it. They were of all shapes and sizes, skin colors and bodily features. There was a chant coming from them—so faint at first, he couldn't make it out. Then he heard it clearly, in unison: *"The divine in me bows to the divine in you."* Joining them, he prostrated himself in supplication before the deity.

Continually chanting the mantra, he dared to look up at the visage above and far off. He opened his mouth to speak platitudes of thankfulness to his idol, but stopped, gaping in bewilderment at what he saw. The face that looked down at him was one of malevolence, not splendor. Its mouth was open as an inverted "v." The round eyes glowed not golden, but with a jaundiced yellow. They were like two dying suns illuminating a dying world with a darkness that masqueraded as light.

At last, Ralph saw through the deception, but he had come to see the movie alone, there was no one to pull him back. The darkness now bathed him and the other worshippers in its false light, a light that was not one of warmth and succor. The light burned; it brought agony; and it never quenched. Ralph could not tell his own pain-filled screams from those of the others with him, echoing for all eternity.

The name on her lapel was "Macy." She had entered theatre four as part of her job to clean up any popcorn, candy wrappers, or other debris left behind by the Hollywood worshipping faithful, while the closing credits rolled on the screen. Looking around, she saw nothing out of order. The seats were all back in place where they should be; the walls were flat in their ancient darkness; the drama masks were settled back into their recesses; and the stringed guide lights were not coiled ready to strike, but in a straight line. She had thought that there was at least one person who had come in to see this showing, but he was nowhere to be seen. Shrugging, she assumed he had left when the film ended, choosing not to watch the credits.

In the large aisle in front of the screen, her foot stepped on something. Picking it up and shining her flashlight, she could see that it was a small metal statue.

215

The gold plating on it was tarnished somewhat, so she could not make out the upside-down "v" of its mouth, or its soulless eyes. She closed her own eyes, clutching the pocket-sized idol in her ebony fingers. For a moment, she thought about her own dreams of being on the big screen one day and then waving to adoring fans while walking on a crimson carpet. This teenage work as an usher was just her start. She adored the movies and thought about the actresses that she could emulate, especially those great, African-American actresses whose movies she had watched, over and over.

Smiling with closed eyes, she clutched the statuette to her chest. She just knew that one day, she would win the prize that all in filmdom crave.

She stuffed the statuette into her trouser pocket and went out to the lobby to collect tickets for the next showing. Fairly skipping, she daydreamed of gold, and of herself bathed in the limelight of Hollywood's glory.

In the corridor, she stopped to see Jeffrey. He said the same words to her that he had spoken on her way in to clean theatre four. "Hello, Macy. Your dark skin looks so pretty. It's like sweet chocolate."

Coming from anyone else, especially some white kid, Macy might've been startled or offended by such a forward comment. But she knew Jeffrey meant no harm by it. He just spoke of things as he clearly saw them through his innocent, slightly out of focus eyes. She knew he had a crush on her and, although she didn't want to encourage him in anyway, she wanted to be kind, and would always take a moment to speak a few words of harmless banter with him in between collecting tickets and cleaning up the theatres.

"Look what I found in the theatre, Jeffrey." She pulled the statuette out of her pocket, and held it out in front, offering it to him to hold.

Jeffrey's face looked lucid and serious again, and his eyes suddenly looked more in focus. He began to look around himself back at theatre four. "Where is the man who went in to see the last show? I didn't see him come out."

"Oh, I don't know, he probably went out one of the side exits, and you just didn't see him leave. There was no one in the theatre when I went in to clean."

"No, no, I would have seen him!"

He looked to Macy as if he were on the verge of panic. It was the first time that she didn't feel comfortable talking to him. "Well, I have to go now, Jeffrey. I have to get back to work. I'll see you later, okay?" She didn't wait for him to answer, but shoved the statuette back into her pocket, and quickly walked away down the corridor.

He turned back to watch her. His look was no longer one of panic, but one of resigned sadness, much the same look he had when Ralph Wagner went by himself into theatre four to watch *Namaste to the Gods*.

She didn't hear him say, "Be careful, Macy. Goodbye."

ABOUT THE AUTHOR

Daniel J. Kaminski and his wife, Vicky, are retired and living in Florida. They have three grown children who are all married and making their way in the world. Dan is the author of a previously published novel, *Small Victories*, available through iUniverse.com. Although residing in Florida, he does not golf, fish, nor own a boat, and he rarely goes in the water because, after all, who knows what kind of horrid beasties are lurking out there. He would much rather spend his time home brewing beer, writing, and reading books by other authors who are so much better at the craft than he is. Contact Dan at djktales@gmail.com, or visit him at FB Daniel Kaminski, or his LinkedIn page.

Printed in the USA
CPSIA information can be obtained
at www.ICGtesting.com
LVHW010407011224
798027LV00002B/408

* 9 7 8 0 9 9 9 8 9 9 3 5 9 *